Sheilah Bain

THE ROUGH ROAD

Winning entry
Scotsman ~~entry~~
                    story
Competition.

              May 1988.

THE ROUGH ROAD

Margaret MacPherson

Illustrated by Douglas Hall

CANONGATE • KELPIES

First published 1965 by Collins
First published in Kelpies 1988
Published In Canada by Optimum Publishing
International (1984) Inc., Montreal

Copyright © 1965 Margaret MacPherson

Cover illustration by Margaret Nisbet

Printed in Great Britain
by Cox & Wyman Ltd, Reading, Berkshire

ISBN 0 86241 177 7

*The publishers acknowledge the financial assistance
of the Scottish Arts Council in the
publication of this volume*

CANONGATE PUBLISHING LTD
17 JEFFREY STREET, EDINBURGH EH1 1DR

Contents

1. Sales Day

Jim edged his way round the group of men clad in oilskins and sou'westers, looking for his friend Tom. What could be keeping him, Jim wondered. How *could* he be so slow on this day of all days, the day of the cattle sale? True, Tom had his father's cattle to bring, but Jim had driven cattle too, and yet he had been waiting a full half-hour already.

It was a terrible day. The wind was blowing half a gale from the west bringing with it a cold, sleety rain which made Jim shiver. It felt more like winter than autumn. The boy turned up the collar of the jacket he was wearing to keep the rain from sliding down his neck as it dripped off his bare head. The jacket had been his foster-father's and was too wide for Jim, who was tall for his thirteen years but very thin. His face, under the mat of dark, straight hair, had a pinched look. His large brown eyes were set deep under very dark brows. He looked like a scarecrow as his clothes flapped wetly in the wind but at least the too-long sleeves of the jacket protected his hands. Not that Jim was in the least put out by his appearance or indeed as much as gave it a thought at that moment for this was a day of excitement. To the boys of the crofting township on Skye an auction sale was as good as a circus is to a town child.

The men hawked and spat. " They should be coming now," they said, searching the road which wound round the head of the loch for a sign of cars, " but likely they'll be late." There was nothing unusual in that for the auctioneers were carrying out a round of sales on the island and each one took a little longer than

7

allowed for. The crofters waited patiently, their backs to the blast, while the dogs crouched at their feet and the cattle bellowed from time to time.

Jim, however, had not learnt patience. He wanted two things; Tom to come, and the sale to start. He kept gazing up the hill but it remained disappointingly empty, all the rest of the men having already arrived with their stock. Snails, he thought bitterly, if they set out at the same time as Tom, would arrive ahead of him! He turned his back and examined the cattle, wondering if the rest were as good as his foster-father's; he thought not. Five minutes crawled by in this fashion and then he allowed himself a glance behind and, oh! cheers, there they were! the beasts plodding slowly towards them with Tom and his father, Murdo Mackenzie, in the rear. He raced to meet them.

" Well, Jim," shouted Murdo above the wind—he was a great big burly man with an air of being never in a hurry—" Sale started? "

" No! But they won't be long now," Jim replied, hope triumphing, and then he whispered indignantly to Tom, "What has been keeping you? Were you carrying the beasts? We've been here for *ages*."

Tom grinned. " And what's the good of that? " he retorted. " You're just getting wet."

" You're not exactly dry yourself! " Jim pointed out. True enough, he wasn't: his blue gaberdine raincoat was soaked through and the wet flaps were rubbing his bare skin behind his knees, making it red and sore. Tom was a solidly built, ginger-headed boy, two months older than Jim. His clothes, unlike Jim's, looked as if they had fitted him at one time, but now his shorts were climbing up his thighs and the sleeves of the jacket up his arms.

This is a story of the nineteen-thirties, when times were bad and shabby children were a common sight. In towns men hung around street corners, workless. They stood in queues to draw the dole, money handed out by the government to keep them and their families from starvation. Sailors hung around the docks hoping to find a ship that wanted men, but more and more ships were being laid up. Shipyard workers stood by the yard gates but the great cranes stood idle. Factory after factory closed down for no one had money to buy their goods. Shopkeepers went bankrupt. Housewives fed their families on bread, margarine and tea. In the country, farmers had to sell their cattle, sheep, and wool, dirt cheap. Some gave up, sold what they had, and left the country; others hung on, waiting for better times, piling up debts even while buying as little as possible.

None of this bothered the boys in the very least as they followed the red, brown, and yellow bullocks to join the others. They stood to leeward of the men and so were sheltered from the worst of the wind and rain.

"Oh! gosh, Tom, I'm hungry," said Jim. He was, in fact, almost always hungry, for his foster-mother judged his appetite by her own and seldom gave him enough to eat.

"Got sandwiches," Tom announced, struggling to pull a packet out of his coat pocket. "Don't know how Mother managed to get them in—I can't get them out!" But at that moment out they came and Tom divided them with his friend. The thick oven scones spread with salt butter and cheese tasted wonderful and were finished all too quickly. Jim's sharp eyes were on the crofters, heads together, talking away ten to the dozen.

"'Terrible weather for September!'" Jim mimicked into Tom's ear. Tom nodded, grinning. "Well! go on. It's your turn now."

Tom reflected. "'Aye, man, terrible! I don't remember the like. Have you cut your corn?'"

Jim giggled, then, straightening his face with an effort, replied dolefully, "'Och! aye, I've cut it and, man, I should have left it the way it was. It's sprouting in the stook and the crows are black on it in the morning'."

9

Tom ran out of invention. "You do it," he said. "I can't copy them the way you do." Thus encouraged Jim gave a very fair imitation of an old man quavering, "'Aye, Tom, man, we'll need to sell every hoof we have for there'll be no harvest this year by the looks of it——'" He broke off suddenly to say in his own voice, "Hie! give me that."

Tom extracted a crust from his pocket. "What are you up to?" he asked. Jim shook his head, snatched the crust, eyed the men's legs, took careful aim, and shied the crust right in among them. At once six collies dived in after it. There were shouts and one yell rose high above the others; the knot of men swayed to and fro, those in the centre struggling to save their legs from the teeth of the dogs, those on the outside pressing in, anxious to see what was going on. Donald Bruce, Jim's foster-father, a man of medium build with a rather flat, weak face, had been bitten in the ankle and was now brandishing his stick and mis-calling the dogs. His brother, Finlay, received a whack on the shin which made him dance round on one leg, clasping the other in both hands. Taller by a head than his brother, he was as lean as a bean pole.

"Can you not look what you're hitting?" he bleated, his Adam's apple wobbling up and down beneath his long blue chin. But Donald wasted no sympathy on him.

"Can you not get out of the way? Didn't the brute's teeth get me in the ankle?" He glared at the dogs still scrapping though the crust of bread had long since vanished and was just about to land another blow on their backs when a shout of, "Here they come!" stopped him.

Jim, hidden behind Tom, was doubled up laughing. "Oh! I got the two of them!" he crowed. "Oh! I got them both."

"Wheest!" whispered Tom, repressively. "They'll hear you if you carry on like that."

But Mr. Blenkinsop, the auctioneer, had arrived.

"Glad to see you, gen'l'm'n!" he said, his bland face beaming from under his peaked cap. " We'd better get down to business straight away. I reckon it's no day for a chat. Make a ring, gen'l'm'n, make a ring, and we'll get started."

The crofters eased out into a circle into which the animals were driven, sometimes one beast at a time on a rope, sometimes as many as six bullocks together, but whatever the number the prices were always low. The same beast would, thirty years on, fetch six times the price it did then. But the sellers had no choice but to sell for with a bad harvest they had no keep for the beasts in the winter. Murdo, Tom's father, sold his fine bullocks for only eight pounds apiece. " Och! you're soft," Donald Bruce told him. " You're just giving them a present!"

" I haven't the feeding for them," replied Murdo in his soft, apologetic voice which sounded so odd coming from his huge barrel of a chest. He had a broad, red face in which eyes, nose, and mouth were crammed into the smallest possible space in the middle. " It's no use taking them home," he added after a pause, but by this time the Bruce brothers were already in the ring. Excitably they kept turning their black bullocks this way and that to show them off to the best advantage. Jim watched intently. He had no love for the Bruces but at that moment felt that their interests were his own. If their cattle topped the sale then Jim could boast of them in school next day. He strained his ears to catch every word of the auctioneer's patter.

" Nice animals, good growthy bullocks—now, what am I bid? Eight pounds? Come along, gen'l'm'n, you won't see the like of these fine beasts every day—" here both brothers nodded vigorously—" seven pounds, then, thank you—seven pounds, I'm bid, seven pounds, ten, eight pounds, thank you, sir, eight pounds, I'm bid, going at eight pounds, going at eight pounds——" Here the nodding was suddenly switched to shakes. " It's a wonder their heads don't roll off!" Tom murmured, but for once Jim was not in sympathy and said, " Hush!"

But not another penny could the auctioneer coax from the buyers, wheedle and cajole them as he might.

"You just come here robbing people!" shouted Donald to no one in particular and Finlay echoed, "Robbing people!"

"It's to my own interest to get every shilling I can for you, Mr. Bruce," the auctioneer said in his bland, syrupy voice. "Bring them back in the spring and they'll make twelve pounds, easy."

"Spring's a long way off!" someone said. "Huh!" was Donald's only comment as he and Finlay drove the scared animals out of the ring through the crowd. Once out, he shouted for Jim. "Here! take them home." With that he hurried back not to miss a minute of the sale. Jim, equally eager, hustled the animals on to the road when they at once moved off homeward of their own accord. Jim slid back beside Tom taking care to keep out of sight of the Bruces. That was easy enough as their eyes were fixed on the ring. Would their neighbour's cattle fetch a higher price than what he, Donald, had refused? It would be a black day, indeed, if the Stewarts could boast that their cattle were the best. In his excitement Donald made chewing motions with his mouth. The heifers, bonny cross-highlanders, made only seven pounds apiece. Donald let out a sigh of relief. Prices had hit rock-bottom. The sale was nearing its end. A big-boned farrow cow was in the ring; its owner, an old man in a tattered coat, a muffler twisted round his scraggy neck, made an outcry when she was knocked down for six pounds.

"You didn't give her a chance!" he kept crying, raising his voice above the screech of the wind. "You knocked her down cheap for a friend of your own. I know your tricks, I'm not so green——"

"Now! Now! Sir," protested the auctioneer, retreating slightly, but his blandness in no way impaired. "Now, now, we've done our best for you. You can see for yourself, the prices are just not in it——"

"I wasn't selling, I wasn't selling!" the old man kept crying.

"You'd no right to knock her down." He shook his fist under
Mr. Blenkinsop's nose. As the auctioneer's retreat was cut
off by the crowd, Jim clutched Tom's arm in keen anticipation
of a fight, but at this point Murdo Mackenzie got hold of the
old man on one side and a man the boys didn't know grasped
his other arm and together they dragged him away from
Blenkinsop and out of the ring.

"I thought he was going to punch him," said Jim. "Pity
your father got him away!"

"The prices are not in it, John!" Murdo kept repeating as the
old man struggled to escape him. "I gave mine away myself
but what could I feed them on?"

"Thieves! Robbers!" shouted old John and suddenly broke

13

off to say in a normal tone of voice, as he gripped the strange man by the hand, " Well! Alasdair, and how are you? You're the big stranger." The stranger was a shortish, thickset chap. In oilskins and sou'wester there wasn't much to be seen of him except a beaky nose and a square chin. He shook the old man warmly by the hand and just then the Bruces came up and joined Murdo. Donald was in fine fettle and kept saying, " I didn't sell! They can't pull the wool over my eyes! I was one too many for them!"

The stranger shot him a keen glance. " Oh, aye! the black bullocks—you refused eight pounds. You were quite right. They'll make you twelve pounds in the spring all right."

Donald was delighted by this. " I was right, wasn't I? I was one too many for them, wasn't I?" he kept repeating.

" If they live to see the spring," said Murdo.

At this the stranger took charge of the weather. " We'll get good days for the harvest yet, never fear. It's only early."

The old man, John Martin, introduced the newcomer as Alasdair MacAskill from Torrin, and they stood chatting while Tom and Jim lingered behind.

But there was nothing more to see, the cattle were being rounded up and driven off, the cars had turned, and the buyers were tumbling back into them, glad to be out of the gale.

" I'd better make tracks," Jim said. " Are you coming, Tom?"

But at this moment Donald turned round as if looking for someone. His eye lighted on Jim.

" Huh! Didn't I tell you to take the cattle home?"

" They went themselves," Jim replied sullenly but Donald had already turned back to the stranger.

" The boy can give you a hand and put you on the right road," he said. " It's a fair step from here."

" That's very kind of you," the man replied. " We'll be seeing you, then, as we're going to be neighbours."

" Aye! Aye! we'll be seeing you," said Donald, grinning all over, and then sharply to Jim, " Stay with Mr. MacAskill and do what he says."

"Be sure and go to the house first, Alasdair," the old man said. " Mary will give you tea. You'll be the better of something."

"Stay with me, Tom!" Jim begged. " I don't know what he's wanting."

" All right! Hold on a minute till I tell Dad."

" We'll have to go back for the cattle, boys," explained the newcomer. " I've got them in the Lodge Park."

Once over the bridge the boys could see that the park was full of cattle—black polls, blue-greys, yellow and brown highlanders with sweeping horns, cross-highlanders, all roans and reds. Jim let out a whistle of surprise. The man glanced at him, amused.

" Aye! they're not bad," he said. "Some of the best cattle in Skye, but we've no time to study them just now for if we don't make a dash for it, we'll be soaked."

The next hail shower was stalking across the loch towards them.

" Quick, boys, run! " And with that he took to his heels up a side road to the door of the nearest cottage just as the first of the hailstones were stotting on the roadway. " No time for ceremony!" the man exclaimed, pushing the door open. All three stood in the narrow passage half taken up with a hallstand, and the two collie dogs crept in to make up the company. Just then a pleasant-looking young woman opened the kitchen door, crying, "Who's there? Come in! Come in! What a terrible day!"

Once he was in the kitchen she recognised her visitor. "Alasdair Bàn!"[1] she cried. " Well, if that isn't a sight for sore eyes. Of course, you'd be at the sale. My! what a day. You're soaked through. Hang your coats in the lobby."

While she was talking the two dogs sneaked into the kitchen.

[1] Bàn means fair.

Alasdair scolded them. "Glen! Spot! Get out of here, you rascals."

"What are you blaming the poor dogs for?" the woman laughed. "You three are just as wet as they are. Goodness me, boys, was it swimming in the sea you were? Come close to the fire. Isn't it lucky I have a good one. I'll soon have something hot inside you."

"We're giving you a lot of bother," said Alasdair.

"Don't tell me you're not hungry! When did you leave home this morning?" she asked the boys.

"About seven," said Tom.

"And not a bite since, I'll be bound! And what were the prices like, Alasdair?" she went on, bustling around preparing a meal.

"Och! the prices were not good at all," he answered sadly.

The woman paused with a spoon in one hand and gave him a sharp look. "And you were buying, I suppose? Trust you, Alasdair, to be on to a good thing."

The man looked a picture of injured innocence. "Do you know this, Mary, if I sold them next week the price would be lower still."

"When will you sell them, then?" she asked as she brewed tea.

"Och! well, I'll need to keep them a year if I want to make anything out of them."

"A year! But your croft's not big enough."

"I haven't got a croft at all which is smaller still." He laughed. "No, but I've taken a grazing, a place called Brae. The Forestry Commission's taken the whole farm there—a waste of good land—and they're going to rent this part to me."

"Brae?" Mary queried. "Where's that, Alasdair?"

"The boys can tell you better than I, for that's where they come from, eh, lads?"

They both nodded. "Brae's over the far side of the loch from us," Tom said.

"You're from Udale, aren't you?" They nodded again. "Goodness gracious, Alasdair, you're not going to bury yourself in Brae at the back of beyond!" exclaimed Mary. "Why, you're always so fond of company."

Alasdair, who had by now taken off his oilskin and sou'wester, rufflled up his fair, wavy hair and looked ruefully at Mary. His eyes were bright blue, set off by dark lashes.

"It's a case of needs must, Mary," he explained. "There's nothing in droving these days. You can buy beasts cheap enough, no doubt about that, but you have to sell them cheaper still. Prices are still falling. I'm planning to keep this lot for a whole year, that is, I'll be selling them in a year's time in October, and if I don't make something out of that, well, that's me finished."

Mary was piling bacon and eggs on to three plates, but Alasdair's remark made her look up, the slice in her hand. "You finished?" she said with all the assurance of an old friend for their two families had lived beside each other when they were children. "*You* won't be finished, not you! Come in to the table, now, boys, I can see you're fair starving and make a good meal. Alasdair, you sit here and make yourself at home."

The boys needed no second telling. They went through those platefuls of bacon and egg like a knife going through butter and then filled up on scones and oatcakes well covered with fresh butter and apple jelly. Alasdair thrust back his chair some time before they did and used the time to fill his pipe.

"Your father wasn't best pleased with the price he got."

"Oh! well, if I didn't forget all about Daisy with you coming in! What did she make?" Alasdair told her what had happened, and Mary was not impressed. "Making an exhibition of himself!" she snorted. "No wonder he's not home yet!"

"Och! don't let on I told you," said Alasdair hastily. "It's hard lines when you think you're not getting a fair chance. Now, boys, if you're ready we'd better be making a start."

"Let them finish their meal, Alasdair, they've a long walk in front of them."

"Oh! I'm just preventing them from bursting," said Alasdair, and then smiled over at Mary. "You were always the one to be looking after lame puppies and lost kittens. Do you remember that blind lamb you had?—Oh! you wouldn't let your brother kill it and when it grew up it was the worst pet I ever saw."

Mary laughed. "I was always looking after something!" she admitted. "And my mother used to get so cross, but I never could bear to see anything cold or hungry or hurt. Are you sure you've had enough, boys?" They nodded.

Mary collected the scraps and put them on the floor but neither dog would go near the plate. "Are they not hungry?" she asked in surprise.

"Oh! they're hungry all right, but I haven't given them leave." He then nodded to the two animals and at once they ate up what was on the dishes.

The boys struggled back into their wet garments, which had been put close to the fire, and followed Alasdair out into the blast after he had thanked Mary warmly for all three. The warmth and comfort of the little kitchen were soon left behind. They rounded up the herd, thirty-six animals in all. The two boys were put to guard the road by which the beasts had come in case any should make a dive for freedom, but as it turned out the dogs did all the work, Glen catching one runaway bullock neatly on the nose and turning it back to the bridge all by himself. Alasdair whistled him in, saying briefly, "Good lad!" The dog leapt up once to lick his master's hand and then dropped back to heel.

The whole drove swept across the bridge spanning the swollen river—the flood water was up nearly to the level of the wooden planks—and then took the road which climbed the hillside above the loch. The three travellers kept their heads down as they faced the full force of the gale and during the showers they had to turn their backs on the worst of its fury. Once they crouched down in a culvert for a moment's shelter. Black clouds scurried over a thick, grey blanket of cloud covering the whole heaven. The hills were lost in scudding mist. The moor lay bleak and sodden to either side of the rough track they were following. There was no sign of man and his works save the occasional peat stack. Now and then a sheep, startled by the dogs, snorted and dashed off into the mist.

They passed the Talisker road. " Is it straight on now to Udale? " the man asked. " Yes! " they both told him.

" Well! we've the wind on our backs now, boys, and I won't say I'm sorry. I've been out on many a bad day but this one would take some beating."

Talking was difficult as the wind blew their words away. The road ran level on the top of the hill for a mile and then descended the far side, keeping well above the river which here ran through a deep, green gorge. As they followed it down, houses grouped round the right-hand side of the loch came into view. Right ahead at the foot of a steep, green hill they could see one small house all by itself.

" That's Brae, isn't it? "

" Yes," said Tom.

" Well, you won't be sorry to get home to-night, boys. Could you give me a hand along the side of the loch or are you too tired? "

Neither boy would admit to being tired. They would go with him as far as he wanted so they helped him turn the whole drove to the left at the bottom of the hill. The dogs forced the tired brutes to cross first one wooden bridge and then a second while torrents of water poured down from the steep hillside.

A cottage stood on the right-hand side of the road and from it a man came running with a coat thrown over his head.

" You've come! " he exclaimed, shaking MacAskill by the

hand. " My word! what a day, man. You'll need to come straight back here and get dried. Don't think of staying in Brae to-night. The wife's expecting you."

" Thank you kindly," Alasdair replied. " We'll just put the beasts up, then—we won't be long."

" You're lucky to have helpers! " the head forester, Charles Grant, remarked, looking at the drover's two bedraggled companions.

" I am that," agreed Alasdair heartily. They pressed on, the road becoming a track with grass growing high on both sides. The herd strung out into a long line. Below the track the ground fell steeply to the shore where the wind was busy lashing the waves on to the rocks. Now and then spindrift rose in a great spiral and fell as salt spray on to the land. When they had marched for almost a mile it was possible to see how the loch turned a little farther on at a right angle from its upper course. A little farther still and the drover made out the angry waters of the Minch as they foamed on to the western coast of Skye.

They reached a point where the path they had so far followed forked, the one branch descending to shore level and the other sloping up the flank of the hill. " Well, now, boys, you know this place and I don't. Would we be better to go up or go down ? "

Tom said they should go down. They could leave the herd on a flat near the Corry Mor river which lay ahead but Jim, stammering a little in his excitement, argued that the other path was better for after half a mile or less it dipped into a corry which would shelter the herd from the worst of the storm.

Alasdair nodded. The boy, for all he looked such a scarecrow and acted dumb, had a head on his shoulders. The dogs got the stragglers under control and the whole herd plodded wearily up the hillside. But it was not far from there. Soon the leaders were above the Corry Mor and began to break off of their own accord, seeing where shelter lay. The corry was a huge basin set in the hills and was the most sheltered spot they could have found for the cattle that wild autumn evening.

Alasdair took it all in at a glance and halted. "We don't need to walk another step, boys," he said. "This is just grand, they'll find their own shelter now."

Then Alasdair, like a yacht tugging a couple of skiffs after it, battled back against the storm to reach Grasco where the forester's house was. There he searched in his pockets for a tip for his helpers and gave them half a crown each, which was real wealth. "Hurry on home," he said, "and change your clothes." The boys muttered a thank you and shuffled off.

"Oh! gosh, I'm tired," said Tom. "It'll be grand to be home."

But Jim was never pleased to go home. The lively look he had worn all day vanished but he said nothing.

"See you to-morrow!" Tom said as he left Jim at his house. It was a stone bungalow with a roof of corrugated iron painted green at some time but the paint had now worn off, showing rusty patches like a skin disease. Jim went round to the back and entered the scullery. He was standing there dripping on to the stone floor and struggling to open the jacket buttons with his numbed fingers when the kitchen door opened and his foster-mother stood looking at him, her thin face expressionless.

"You're home," she said.

Jim looked at her. No! No! I am not home, I have no home to go to.

For a moment he thought he had said the words aloud or that she could read them in his heart but her expression did not change. She waited.

"Yes," he said, his fingers busy with the buttons. "Yes, I'm home."

2. A Fight

Next morning Donald and Finlay Bruce were having breakfast at the small deal table which stood against the wall opposite the fire. Finlay was spooning porridge into his cavern of a mouth and Donald was tapping the top of his egg.

" Tcha! " he exclaimed angrily, pushing the plate away from him.

" What's the matter, dear? " cried his wife, Sarah.

" Hard-boiled! "

" Oh! no, dear, I gave it just three minutes and a half, three minutes and a half I gave it."

" You know I won't eat a hard-boiled egg," replied her husband crossly. " Give it to the boy. Pour me out a cup of tea."

Sarah, tall, thin, and dried-up looking, hurried to the fire for the tea-pot and scurried back to pour out a cup for her husband. Finlay's egg was not hard-boiled and he guessed that he had been given his brother's by mistake, but he said nothing. With a bit of luck he might get the other egg as well. It was worth singing dumb, anyway.

Jim, meanwhile, was seated on the wooden settle beneath the window. A large creeping plant on the window sill blocked the view. It never produced a flower, disheartened, perhaps, by the general gloom. Jim nipped a few leaves off when his foster-mother's back was turned and then stared for the thousandth time at the large picture which hung high on the wall above the table. It was crowded with people all in long clothes but the thing which puzzled Jim was the fact that a dog was lying quietly beside several very fat sheep. Never in his life had he seen such a thing. The picture was called "Peace." His eyes went back to the table. His uncle was finishing his last scone. In another moment both had risen and crossed over to the fire. Jim sidled into Finlay's chair. He could not take his eyes off the egg which Finlay, after all, had not dared to touch. Now Sarah's thin hand covered it.

"If you had been a good boy last night," she said to Jim, fixing her dark eyes on him, "you would have got it." Jim scowled and looked at his plate. "But you were not a good boy," went on his foster-mother, enjoying herself, "so we'll put the egg up there." She crossed to the dresser and placed the boiled egg, still in its wooden holder, on the highest shelf. "If you had been a good boy——" she repeated and then paused.

"What's he done now?" demanded her husband, realising a little late that he was expected to play his part.

"What has he done?" asked Sarah dramatically. "What does he ever do but tell lies?" Jim squirmed on his seat. Let her get on with it and then give him his breakfast.

"Huh!" grunted Finlay, who liked to join in and who still had an interest in the egg. "You shouldn't do that."

"Told me lies," said Sarah, getting into her stride, "and bad boys don't get eggs."

"What was he lying about this time?" asked Donald, not that he was greatly interested, but in duty bound.

"He told me last night that the drover gave him no money and what did I find——" Here Donald interrupted, interested at last. "The drover? Oh, aye, MacAskill—that's a chap that knows what he's talking about, told me I'd done the right thing by not selling. Well, what did he give you, Jim?"

"Half a crown," muttered Jim sullenly. He had tried hard to keep the coin from Sarah and had hidden it in the toe of his boot but she had been one too many for him.

" So well he might, seeing you had a long walk——" Donald began, and then saw by a side glance at Sarah that he was on the wrong tack. " Aye, but you'll be wanting boots soon enough, telling us that pair's too small so you'd better be helping to pay for them."

" When I was your age I never had boots at all, just my bare feet, and the snow on the ground," said Finlay.

" Young people think they can have everything for the asking," said Sarah, " but money doesn't grow on bushes."

Oh! gosh, thought Jim, will they never stop! But as his porridge was now on the table he didn't waste time talking. He had to eat as much as possible in a short time. This wolfing horrified Sarah. " Eat us out of house and home, you will! I've never seen anyone eat like you."

" And that's true," agreed her husband. " I'm sure I never saw his like, either."

" Uh-huh! " was Finlay's contribution, but it came out with a wealth of feeling.

" For ten years we've kept you on the very best and all the gratitude you show is to tell me lies."

Jim shut his ears to the hail of words. It had been much worse last night when, tired out, he had been alone with Sarah. She had frightened him then. It was the way she looked at him, just sat silent and looked at him. He would do anything just to get her to stop. But with the men there and in the light of day rows like this were just the normal pattern of living, no more to be worried about than hail showers or the belt at school.

Sarah, having drunk one cup of tea and eaten one slice of bread and butter, began to clear the table. This habit of hers explained Jim's haste. He had seldom time to eat all he wanted. The two men were muttering over the fire. Jim pricked up his ears: " Keep at home—do some work, a bit of drying——" and understood that they were thinking of keeping him off school to help in the harvest. Not to-day, he thought, he wanted to talk over the sale with Tom and boast to the rest of what he had seen and done, so, with the skill of long practice, he had taken his school satchel and was away before they knew what was happening.

He was late, he'd have to run. The wind still blew but less fiercely, the clouds were still flying past but through their ragged fleeces patches of blue sky were appearing. He kept looking across the loch to Grasco but not a beast was to be seen. They'll be still snug in the Corry Mor, he guessed. Rounding the last bend, he saw Bella Ross and her younger sister, Katie-Ann, a little ahead. This made him slacken his pace for he had no wish to walk with Bella, who was always giggling, nor yet with Katie-Ann, who turned on the water-works for the least trifle.

School was held in a room which had once been the gun-room of the shooting lodge. It was dark and gloomy, as its only window faced east, the walls were varnished, and heavy oak desks took up all the floor space. Tom and Jim, being the oldest pupils, shared a desk in the back row. That morning the boy could not concentrate on his lessons, he was perpetually whispering to Tom about the events of the day before.

Finally Miss Menzies lost her temper. " You will stay in the classroom during the break," she snapped. " I won't have this kind of behaviour. You are in school to-day, not at a sale." Miss Menzies was a brisk young woman who could handle a strap so that it hurt. Jim was disappointed. He had meant to play auctioneer during the break. " Seven pound I'm bid, seven pounds, gen'l'm'n, come along, now, a nice young heifer, seven pound, half a crown, thank you, and five shillings and ten." He stood by himself in the classroom and held the auction sale all on his own but it would have been more fun with the rest looking on. Still he could do it at dinner time if the rest didn't take too long over their dinner. Jim stayed at school and ate a piece of bread which he had managed to slip into his pocket. He loitered about the back of the school, perched himself on a stone which did duty for the auctioneer's stance, and once more sold imaginary cattle to imaginary buyers. " Grand beasts from our well-known customer, Mr. Bruce, good growthy bullocks——" But as he was all alone, the game palled and he looked about for something else to do. It was then he saw Donnie's football lying by the barn door. It wasn't much of a football, it needed pumping, but it was better than nothing. Jim gave himself headers against the barn wall. Donnie was Tom's younger brother and there was no love between him and Jim. From the earliest days Donnie had been held up to Jim as an example to be copied. " See how neatly Donnie does his sums. Why can't you do your sums like that? Look how neatly Donnie covers his books. Why can't you keep your books as neatly as that?" And Donnie would smirk and give himself airs.

Jim suddenly remembered the drover's cattle. The Lodge was a high, gaunt, stone building, the last in the township. A few tall trees grew in front in the overgrown garden and blocked the view. Jim, therefore, picked up the ball and walked to a spot clear of the house where he could see the far side of the loch, but no cattle were there.

" Jim! Jim! give me my ball."

Now Jim had really intended to play at cattle sales when the other children came back but when he heard Donnie's angry cry he was seized with the idea of teasing him and began running with the ball. " Come and get it!" he shouted. Then began a game of running and dodging, Jim laughing and Donnie fretting. " It's *my* ball, you've no right to go off with my ball."

This only encouraged Jim. " Come on!" he mocked. " You're so clever, come and get your beautiful ball—clever boy!" He flung the ball ahead and raced after it, catching it again before Donnie could reach it.

" I'll never let you play with my ball again!" cried Donnie, red in the face and breathless. " Tom! Tom! you take it from him."

A Fight

"Come on, Jim, give it to Donnie, we can all have a game," urged Tom, but Jim was enjoying his own game and had no intention of stopping. At last the younger boy hurled himself on to Jim and they both fell on the wet ground, rolling over and over, Donnie grabbing any bit of Jim he could hurt and Jim fighting silently to get on top. His weight told in the end and he straddled the luckless Donnie, holding his arms stretched above his head on the grass and saying over and over, "I *will* have the ball, I *will* have the ball, you can't keep it from me!"

"Stop it, Jim, let him get up!" pleaded Tom, and the girls were gawping at the two muddy, blood-stained figures when a sharp voice cut in.

"What's all this? You again, Jim Smith? I might have known it. Let that boy up at once! You're nothing but a bully, fighting a boy two years younger than yourself." It was Miss Menzies, their teacher. At the sound of her voice Jim scrambled to his feet. Miss Menzies gave Donnie a helping hand. Blood was running down his cheek but he was doing his best not to cry.

"What were you fighting about?" the teacher asked. The boys said nothing, but the girls rushed in: "Please, Miss, it was about the ball. Jim Smith took it and, please, Miss, it's Donnie's ball."

Miss Menzies cast a last withering glance in Jim's direction as she helped Donnie towards the house. "What you need is a good thrashing!" she threw over her shoulder. "And I'll tell Donnie's father what you've been doing."

"O-o-h! Jim Smith, you'll catch it now," chorused the girls, "and a good thing, too. We won't be sorry for you!" Jim made a half-hearted lunge in their direction but Tom pulled him away. "Och! don't mind for them, Jim, they're only a lot of sillies. Come down to the shore till I clean you up."

Jim winced as the salt water nipped his cuts and scratches.

He wriggled in his friend's grasp, complaining, "Oh! you're hurting me, Tom, oh! stop that, for goodness' sake."

But Tom persisted. "Losh! stand still, man, I must get the blood off you." He dipped his dirty handkerchief once more in the sea and resumed his task. "She'll be wild if you go back to school looking like that!"

"What's the odds? She's wild, anyway, whatever I do. *He* jumped on me, anyway—I was only running with the ball. I could have stayed off school to-day, too, they were thinking of cutting corn—wish to goodness I had."

"Aye! Dad was saying we might do a bit in the evening as it's drying up."

"I hate corn, I hate hay, I hate everything on the croft!" exclaimed Jim passionately. "Scraping and scratching away every day in the year like a lot of hens on a midden and nothing to show for it at the end of it all—not even a decent price for a good beast. When I grow up I'll have lots and lots of cattle," he concluded illogically.

"If you do, you'll have to feed them," Tom pointed out. "They won't live on air."

"*He's* got lots of cattle and no corn!" retorted Jim with a wave of his arm in the direction of Brae.

"I bet he'll give them something in the winter," Tom answered, gazing across the water, "only, he's got lots and lots of ground——"

"Yes, hasn't he?" Jim replied eagerly. "And did you ever see such grass! There hasn't been a beast on it for the last six months. It was great yesterday, wasn't it, driving all those beasts, and his dogs were great, I've never seen a dog as clever as Glen."

"I'd have liked it fine if it hadn't been so wet," said Tom. Jim gave a snort of irritation but just at that moment the school bell went and they had to hurry to stand in line. Afternoon school droned along till four o'clock.

A Fight

When they trooped out of the dark classroom the sunshine seemed quite dazzling by contrast. There was no hope of football that evening as most of the children would have to work on the crofts. Jim dawdled along on his way home. No doubt the men would have been cutting corn all day and Sarah binding the cut corn into sheaves. His job would be to lift the sheaves and make stooks of them. He kicked the stones on the road and wished that he was anywhere but where he was. He came in sight of the house and quite suddenly his conduct changed. From a saunter, his walk changed to a run, for there, lying on the front step of the cottage lay Glen, his coat as bushy as ever, his short black and brown nose resting on his forepaws.

"Glen!" said Jim softly. The dog gave one wag of his tail, a mere acknowledgment that they had once met. Jim could hear voices coming from the kitchen. He went round the back of the house and came upon Spot with his nose in a bucket. Hearing footfalls the dog leapt away. "Spot! Spot!" Jim

called coaxingly. Spot came up to be petted but his mind was clearly on what he could find to eat so, having given Jim a quick lick, he disappeared behind a shed to forage. Jim slipped into the scullery as quietly as a shadow. He could make out Alasdair's voice, then there came a burst of laughter, an unusual sound in that house. Under cover of the noise Jim pushed open the door and sidled on to the nearest chair.

"Is it yourself, Jim?" said Alasdair in his easy, kind way. "None the worse of your wetting yesterday?" Jim shook his head. "Well, it was a coarse day and no mistake," Alasdair went on. "The boys were a great help, especially your Jim, for it was his idea to put the beasts in the Corry Mor. It was the best possible place and they never stirred out of it till this afternoon."

Donald, surprised by this testimonial, gazed at Jim as if he had never seen him before. Finlay grunted, which committed him to nothing if Sarah cared to take the matter up later on. She contented herself at that moment by lifting a plate of soup and putting it down in front of the boy. This prompt service astonished Jim and the only person unaware of anything odd was the visitor himself. He went back to what they had been talking about when Jim came in. "Indeed, I mind your father fine," he said to Sarah. "He was a fine figure of a man even when I met him and he was old then and he kept some very nice cattle. I bought some stirks off him that back-end and my word! prices were high, three times what they are now. I didn't see you that time though your mother took me into the house and gave me tea."

"I'm sure you would see Anna, my sister, she was at home then," said Sarah, delighted to talk of her old home. "She's in service in Oban now, one of the best of hotels! Ah! she's the lucky one, no hard work binding the corn for Anna!"

Donald grunted and scraped out the bowl of his pipe with

his knife. Alasdair changed the subject. " They're good crofts, these ? "

" Oh, aye, good enough, they carry four cows and their followers," said Donald, glad to get away from Sarah's family, " and a horse and there's the share in the sheep stock over and above that."

" Och! the sheep," lamented Sarah. " What is it but robbery, expenses all the time and the shepherd's wages for doing nothing, and dip and bottles of whisky for the shearing and at the end of the year there's nothing left to divide—they've taken it all ! "

" Och! the prices are poor," said Donald hastily. " Look at them yesterday! No price for a grand beast and it's the same with the sheep. Cheviot wool at tenpence the pound. What's that but robbery? The boy's finished his soup, wife."

" Finished already ?" Sarah began, then recollecting they had company she added, " Well, I've a nice piece of salt mutton I kept for him." She fished it out of the soup pot and with her back to Alasdair cut Jim a very small slice, but even so Jim counted himself lucky. Without Alasdair he wouldn't have smelt meat. Potatoes by themselves would have been his share.

" Hurry up, now," said his foster-father, " and away and make the stooks." But Jim chewed every mouthful for full value and swallowed each reluctantly.

There was some more talk about people they all knew and then Alasdair came round to the purpose of his visit. He had some gear to ferry across to Brae and he had heard that the Bruces had a boat. He had scarcely got the word " boat " out of his mouth when there was a rapid fire of disclaimers and much head shaking. "Boat!" cried Donald, leading off. Well! they had had a boat, sure enough, but she was in no fit state to take anyone's goods. It would be no kindness to lend any man such a vessel. It was risking a man's life to go out in her, chimed in Finlay, risking one's life, she wasn't a boat at all, just a sieve.

Alasdair was just going to get up and say he would try somewhere else when Jim broke in eagerly:

" The boat's all right! You were out in it last week! It'd carry the gear fine." There was a strained silence in the little kitchen. Into the horrid pause the ticking of the clock on the dresser sounded as loud as the trump of doom. Then all three broke out at once. The boat *had* been all right, they had been out in her, but the gale had thrown her over on her side and one of her planks had been stove in. If they had had a boat, a seaworthy boat, wouldn't Alasdair have had the use of it at once? But, of course, the boy hadn't known.

" She was all right two days ago! " Jim persisted. " I'll go and have a look."

" You will not! " cried Donald furiously, getting to his feet. " You get out of here and lift those sheaves like I told you." He stood glaring at Jim who understood it was time to be off. " If you want a boat," Donald went on to the drover, " you'll get a good one from Murdo Mackenzie. His is the last house, the Lodge."

" Haven't they everything? " said Sarah, sitting down and rocking herself backwards and forwards. " The best house and the best steading, a horse and a plough, and the teacher lodging with them. They're well off—the Mackenzies! "

Alasdair made his escape as quickly as he could. Oof! he had certainly put his foot in it that time! It was no use trying to borrow from the Bruces, that was crystal clear. Poor Jim! He hoped they wouldn't give him a telling off when he got home. The lad hadn't meant any harm.

Jim, from his post up in the corn field, kept a watch on the loch. As far as he could see no boat put out from the little port beyond the graveyard. But he took no comfort from that for he was sure they would go. If there was any fun to be had he was sure to miss it. That horrid boy, Donnie, would be allowed to go to Brae or Tom and Tom hadn't enjoyed driving the cattle half as much as Jim had. But it was always the way. Why did the Bruces have to refuse everyone everything? There was nothing wrong with the boat! Talk about telling lies! In his exasperation he kicked a clod of earth with his boot, kicked and kicked till it crumbled into fragments. A small stone landed on a nearby potato shaw and a black hen jumped out, squawking loudly. In a flash Jim was on his knees, peering under the shaws.

Six white eggs met his delighted eyes. He looked all round—no one! He took one egg, cracked it, and poured the contents down his throat, then another. He hesitated over a third and then decided to store his find. He pulled the withered shaws back over the nest till not a glint of white showed, then he buried the broken shells. He'd make a fire on Saturday or Sunday or the first day he had time and he'd cook the others in an old tin. He might share them with Tom but Tom got plenty of eggs at home. His best plan would be to eat the lot himself.

3. Over to Brae

A few days after that when the children came running out of school they saw Murdo standing in the yard. He had his little black mare, Sally, yoked in the cart and shouted to Tom to come and hold her head. Jim hung around, curious to know what was going on. Tom fondled Sally's nose and whispered stories into her ears. In a few minutes Murdo reappeared with Alasdair Bàn. They were carrying the spring of a bed between them.

"It's a wee bit awkward," said Murdo, resting the end of the spring on the ground and eyeing the cart. "Maybe we'd be as well to take the back off it."

"Aye! just as well," agreed Alasdair. "Oh! hallo, boys, you can give us a hand to the beach."

Then began a hurrying, a bustling, and scurrying in all directions such as was most uncommon in Udale. A mattress, bags, boxes, dishes, a frying pan all on its own, two pots, rabbit traps, a spade, a bundle of blankets done up in a torn tarpaulin were only a few of the items handled that busy evening. Alasdair kept giving orders and the entire Mackenzie family kept running. There were five of them: Tom, Donnie, Mary, aged ten, Susan, five, and wee Nan, three and a half years old. The last two kept getting in the way.

"Oh! keep them away from the cart!" their mother cried. "That mare's not safe."

Alasdair picked up one in one hand and the other in the other and held them aloft. The little girls giggled with pleasure.

34

" You'll come to Brae with me," he said, " and be my little sweethearts." Susan, black-haired and rosy-cheeked, was all for it but Nan wriggled down and back to her mother.

" One's enough for you! " Murdo's wife, Effie, said, laughing. " But, oh! Alasdair, you'll die in that place all by yourself."

" What! me, an old sailor? I'll manage fine."

" What if you fall ill? "

" I'll wave a sheet and my friends here—" he nodded to Tom and Jim—" will come over and rescue me."

" It's all very well to laugh," Effie rebuked him, " but you could break a leg out on the hill and how would anyone know? "

" There was always someone living out there, wife," said Murdo. He kept eyeing the load in the cart apprehensively and saying, " Maybe we have enough! " His wife kept arriving with little parcels, scones in one, a pound of fresh butter in another, some potatoes in a sack, and half a dozen eggs, for she had taken the newcomer under her wing and felt that all those gifts were not too much for a man going to face the wilderness. But Alasdair was whistling cheerfully as he tied ropes to secure the load.

" Now, have we got everything, do you think? " he asked as he came out from under the cart. " I'm sure there was something else——"

" The paraffin! " exclaimed Effie. " Remember we put it in the shed to be well away from the food. Jim, run and fetch it and carry it yourself in case it spills, nasty, smelly stuff! "

Jim ran to the shed. He was delighted that he had been given something to look after. Perhaps they'd let him go over to Brae if he hung on to the paraffin the whole way. He need not have worried. Alasdair knew the value of willing helpers and also, to his cost, the steepness of the path up to the Brae cottage from the shore.

At last they were off, the cart lurching over the rough ground past the old graveyard with its tall trees, and on out to the shore.

The tide was high and there rode the *Seagull*, George's and Dan's big boat in which they fished for lobsters round the coast. Wading out in their fishermen's thigh-length boots they loaded the boat with the gear which the others carried from the cart. With so many helping, the cart was soon empty and the boat full. Jim went aboard, still hugging the paraffin flask. He and Tom made their way to the prow and sat there resting after all the bustle. It was a calm and lovely evening. The shore they were leaving was already in shadow but the sun was shining full on Brae and on Ben Mor, the beautiful, conical hill which rose behind the house. The *Seagull* moved out into the loch, gathering speed. The bow wave curled back and broke into two white wings. A cormorant flew low over the water and a little black guillemot bobbed up and down quite close till it decided suddenly it was too close for comfort and dived.

Jim lay scanning the hillside for cattle. He could make out a group grazing near the Corry Mor burn and some more close to the house which was rapidly drawing near so that the boys could now make out the large windows staring sightlessly at them. George eased off the engine as they nosed their way in beside a natural jetty formed by a long black shelf of rock projecting out into the loch. Dan had dropped an old lorry tyre over to protect the boat's side and now came forward, gripped the rock, and held on.

The boys were on their feet ready to jump.

" Careful! " Dan cautioned them. They landed safely.

" Put a turn of rope round that rock, Tom! " Alasdair shouted, " and that'll leave us all free to unload."

Jim had already carried his precious paraffin to a safe place and now ran back to help.

" Pile everything up on the rocks just now, boys. We don't want to be keeping George and Dan from their creels."

" Oh! time enough," replied George. " Can we give you a hand with the heavier stuff? "

" No, no, you've given me a grand hand already. I'd have taken six or seven trips to carry all that with a rowing boat."

" Are the boys staying with you? "

" Aye! Aye! Can you call for them on your way back? "

" Surely, but we'll be a while."

" And so will we getting all this to the top! "

The *Seagull* reversed slowly till clear of the rock, then turned and made out to sea.

A furious burst of barking came from the house.

" We had enough to ferry without *them*! " commented Alasdair, pushing his fair hair back from his brow. " Well, now, shipmates, what shall we take first? "

" The food," said Jim.

" The pots and pans," said Tom.

Alasdair laughed, and gave his head a final scratch before replacing his cap back to front.

" Here am I trying to do with as little as possible and just look at it! " he said, surveying the pile ruefully. " Tell you what, boys, I'd best get the worst over first while I have my strength. See and hoist the meal bag on my back and then take whatever you fancy but don't strain yourselves—you're young yet and must take care." It was as much as the boys could do to heave the 140-lb. bag on to Alasdair's shoulders and he staggered off under the burden, his legs trembling.

" It's some weight," said Tom. " Do you think he'll manage? " Jim nodded. He was sure he would.

The worst part of the business was balancing on the rough shore. Tom took a box and Jim tackled the big bundle of blankets. This seemed quite light at the bottom of the hill and heavy as lead by the time he reached the top. Alasdair was just ahead, bent forward. With a sigh of relief he dropped the bag on to the topmost step leading to the tiny porch. " Och! that's not good for a man, straining the heart! " he remarked as he wiped sweat from his face, then mounted the steps and opened

the door. At once the two dogs bounded out, narrowly missing their master and knocking Jim clean over as he rounded the corner. For his part he lay where he had fallen on top of the blankets which was fine and comfortable while he listened to Alasdair abusing the dogs, but a sharper cry brought him scrambling to his feet only to find that the culprit was Spot who had been about to lift his leg against the bundle. "The dirty brute. Are you hurt? No? Good enough, come in, then, come in, and you're very welcome to Brae." This was said as regally as though Brae were a mansion and not a three-roomed corrugated iron hut. "I'll take the blankets. Aye! there's a weight in them; you did well carrying them up."

The room they entered was oblong in shape and would have been very dark but for the evening sun shining in. The walls and even the ceiling were stained dark brown and varnished. It had two windows, one looking out to sea and the other on to the hill. A small peat fire smouldered in the grate.

" Well, boys, what do you think of this for a home ? " They stood looking in silence which made Alasdair continue hastily. " Och! you wait till we make it ship-shape; it'll be as snug a little berth as any man could want. Just you wait and see." He was reassuring himself as much as the boys. He went down on one knee by the fire and taking peats from a box, broke them over his other knee and placed small bits round the core of the fire which he blew on till it burst into flames. At once the bare, sombre room became more home-like. Alasdair gave the kettle a shake. " Empty! Away to the well, Tom, and fill it. Aye! the well's just round the corner of the house on that side and a fine, handy place for a well to be." Tom came back in a minute with the kettle full of water and Alasdair slung it on the hook above the fire. " Now! " he said, " that'll be boiling by the time we're ready for it so off we go again, boys! "

The thought of food was cheering, especially to Jim who had had nothing but a couple of pieces since morning. The boys ran down the hill to the shore but they soon became painfully acquainted with every step of the way back, first the rocks and then the pebbly beach, soft marsh ground after that where the long spears of the yellow flags dragged at their legs. Once clear of that they crossed a tiny stream, then the path rose steep as the side of a house. This was the back-breaking part of the business. Lifting each foot became an effort, sweat prickled on their foreheads, their hearts thumped, and the muscles of their legs ached.

" Well! " exclaimed Alasdair as he sat down on a box after their last trip. " You'll not be sorry that's done, eh? It wouldn't do to flit every day."

"It's steep," said Tom. No one wished to dispute that statement for a moment. Jim was wistfully eyeing the kettle but it was Spot who drove his master to action for he was hopefully sniffing a bag of scones.

"You greedy hound!" shouted Alasdair. "Out you go!" The dog slunk out, tail between his legs.

"But he didn't touch the food the day of the sale," Jim said.

Alasdair snorted. "Because I had my eye on him! I got him when he was six months old and if you ask me they starved him for I've never been able to give him his bellyful. I'll need to put all the food into the back room till I've time to put up shelves. Now, if I had only Glen I could leave the food here right in the middle of the floor and he wouldn't go near it, but I had him as a puppy." Glen, on hearing his name, wagged his tail gently but did not stir from where he lay in a corner with his head on his paws. "Now, boys, look for the tea and we'll need cups. Which of you can lay his hand on the sugar?"

Then began a search for everything. Tom was sure the tea was in one box and Jim was sure it was in another and Jim was right. Alasdair turned a packing case upside down to serve as a table. "Put all the food you can find on that, Jim." He made the tea and Tom succeeded in finding three cups.

"Well, now, boys," said Alasdair, regarding their joint efforts with satisfaction, "this is a bit of all right. No knives? I've my pocket knife here, we can use it in turn." He wiped the blade of the knife on his trousers and they set to on the feast and for ten minutes or so ate in silence. When Alasdair had had enough he lit his pipe and threw more peat on the fire making the firelight dance over the dark walls. "Well! I was lucky coming to a place where the man before me cut peat and hay before he went and left them to me as a kind of legacy."

"Is there hay?" asked Tom in surprise.

"Aye, is there, the barn along there is full of it. That's where

I've been sleeping till I could get the bed across and it wasn't a bad sleeping place either barring the noise the mice made. Well, Tom, if you've had enough, maybe you could give me a hand with the bed. No, don't hurry yourself, Jim, Tom and me will manage fine."

The two of them manœuvred the spring into the front bed-room where Jim joined them and helped by holding the foot of the bed till Alasdair got the spring into place. Together they dragged through the big mattress and Alasdair flung the bundle of blankets on top. "There!" he remarked. "You won't get many bedrooms with a view like that right down the loch to your houses."

"You can't see our house," said Tom.

"No, Aird Point hides it, but I can see Jim's. You'll be able to see my light at night and that puts me in mind I'd better fill the lamp. I've been making do with candles but they're chancy things and could easily put the place on fire."

The new lamp was in a box with the dishes. It was made of blue glass and had a double wick. Alasdair filled it carefully out-side on the rough path and when he came in put a match to both wicks but left them very low.

"We'd need a lamp to see this one by!" he joked. "But if I have to walk seven miles for a lamp glass I'll have to be careful."

"The boat's coming!" Tom, who had stayed outside, called.

"We'll go down then," said Alasdair. "You've been a great help, boys, and I'll be pleased to see you any time you care to come up."

The fishermen refused to go up to the house that night, they would visit him some other time. Alasdair repeated his thanks and stood watching them as they moved out. For a little while they could make out his lone figure on the rock but then the dusk swallowed him up.

"He'll not stay long alone in Brae," said George. Dan grunted assent.

"Oh! he will!" exclaimed Jim. "It's a grand place and he's going to make it ship-shape." The fishermen were not much given to talking and they said nothing more till they reached the point. "The tide's out, boys," they explained. "We can't take you any farther in. Can you manage from here?"

Tom said they would manage fine but Jim did not feel so cheerful. He had listened to too many ghost stories round the fire at night and up till now had never willingly gone out in the dark alone. He hurried after Tom who seemed to have cat's eyes and kept to the narrow track without difficulty. He began whistling. "Oh! don't, Tom," Jim implored him, stumbling over a stone in his hurry to keep up.

"Don't what?"

"Don't whistle!"

"Why ever not?"

"They might hear you."

"Who's they?"

"Fine you know!" said Jim indignantly. "And we're going past *their* place."

To Jim's disgust Tom burst out laughing. "Is it ghosts you mean, man? There's no such thing! You've been listening to Kursty Morag's yarns—she's champion—but it's all rot. Why, we've lived close to the graveyard for years and we've never seen a thing."

"They mightn't come after you!" Jim pointed out.

This did not please Tom one bit. "Why wouldn't they? We're as good as you, aren't we?"

"Och! yes, but——"

"Of course they'd come after us if they were *there*, stupid! But they're not there. Dad says it's all super—super—well, super-something."

"You don't even know the word!" Jim mocked.

" Well! I'll show you, then." By now the two boys were level with the graveyard at a place where the high wall was tumbling down. Tom ran over and scrambled up the fallen stones till he stood perched on top. He cupped his hands to his mouth and shouted, " Come on! Chase me! I'm here! "

The elm tree branches stirred slightly. The place below was a pool of darkness except where white lichen on stones gleamed faintly. Jim, too frightened to move, expected to see Tom snatched into a grave before his very eyes.

" See that now——! " Tom began when there came an eldritch screech just beside him. With one bound Tom came off the wall. An owl floated out over their heads. Jim exploded into laughter. " Oh! you were scared, you were scared! Preaching away at me and you're not so brave after all! "

Tom laughed a little ruefully at himself and then said, " But, don't you see, Jim, that's how ghost tales start. If Bella had been here she'd believe she saw, well, anyway, *heard* a ghost, to the end of her days." But he had lost the battle against superstition for that night at least. Jim went on laughing at him to the door of the Lodge.

" Will you come in? " said Tom. Jim hesitated, sorely tempted. There'd be a row at home, that was for sure. He'd taken the whole evening off and a fine evening at that. He hadn't given the matter a thought all afternoon but now the moment of reckoning was upon him.

" I'd better get back. They'll be wondering—there wasn't much drying, was there, Tom? "

Tom gave this his earnest consideration. " No, there wasn't very much, especially if the corn was very wet, it wouldn't dry on a day like this." This was true comfort but Tom's innate honesty made him add, " They might have wanted you to shift the stooks." It was only too likely. Jim's heart did a dive down to his boots. Walking along the road he foresaw his reception, Sarah sitting in the old rocking chair by the fire, the black cat on her knee. She'd egg the men on to belt him. He could see Donald taking off his heavy belt. Jim's breath came faster and his skin prickled. How he hated being hurt! They thought he was tough at school because he never flinched when he got the strap and he'd wink at the class as he went back to his seat. But that was easy because he could play up to the rest. It was a different matter all together alone in that kitchen with that beastly cat purring and making dumplings with its paws on Sarah's black skirt and Sarah's queer eyes burning right through him; well, he wasn't brave then. As he thought of all this his pace slowed to a crawl. It was the not knowing, too. Sometimes when he had screwed himself up to face the worst nothing happened and other times when he thought everything was all right he walked straight into a row. In sight of the house at last he could see light shining from the kitchen window. Funny! Sarah always drew the curtains as soon as she lit the lamp and even before she turned the wick up because, she said, people looked in. When he reached the back door Ben, the old sheep dog, barked. Jim stood silent in the scullery, afraid to open the kitchen door. Donald did it for him. "Who's there?" he shouted. "Oh! it's you, is it? Just you come in here and tell us what you've been up to."

"I was at the Lodge."

"What were you doing there?"

"Playing."

"Playing!" cried Donald with a wealth of scorn. "Playing at this time of night!"

"At this time of night!" echoed Finlay, and they both glared at him. But Sarah wasn't there so Jim took heart.

"There was no drying," he declared. "I'd have come straight home if there'd been drying." This took the two men by surprise and they were almost appeased till they remembered they had had the stooks to shift by themselves and the cows to fetch home for milking.

"You'll come straight home after this!" cried Donald. "Have we to keep you and feed you for nothing and not a stroke of work out of you?"

"Huh! isn't that it?" cried Finlay. "It's the belt you need."

Jim sensed he was close to danger. "Where's she?" he asked.

"She's in bed, she has a bad head."

Cheers! thought Jim, they won't beat me, it would make too much noise. With a sudden rush of confidence he said, "I'm hungry, is the dinner there?" It was touch and go again. He could feel Donald hesitate. Would he order him off to bed supperless? He would if Finlay got a chance to open his mouth. "There's a potato in the pot," he remarked more coolly than he felt. "I'll just have that." There were indeed two or three potatoes in the pot, rather dried up but still eatable. Jim carried them over on a plate to the table. When fetching a fork from the drawer in the dresser it was easy to take a slice of butter from the dish. He sat with his back to the men, mashed his potatoes till the melted butter ran all through them and ate them up with relish. Two meals and no punishment! He wasn't doing too badly.

4. Sunday Visit

Alasdair had given the boys on the day of the flitting an invitation to pay him a visit at any time. It was an invitation which Jim longed to accept but shyness kept him back. What if he went up and found Alasdair out? Then he wouldn't be able to go again, or so he felt. Worse still, what if he went and Alasdair didn't really want him? He might even send him home and faced with such a prospect Jim preferred to stay away. But at the same time he longed to go. Into his dull existence the stranger with his herd of cattle and his dogs had come like a breeze of wind into a stuffy room. Now he did not want to lose sight of him. When at school he kept straining his eyes to catch a glimpse of him turning the cattle back from the forestry drains whenever they had wandered too far down the lochside. Now and then he had glimpses of Alasdair, leaning on his tall stick, talking to a neighbour and always giving the impression that they had been bosom friends all their lives. If at such times Alasdair noticed Jim he would give him a friendly smile and say, "Well, Jim, lad, and how's the world treating you?" but Jim was too shy to stand and talk. His legs hurried him past even while he longed to stay.

One Sunday morning Finlay said, "Don't go off now, boy! You're to herd the cows beside the corn for an hour. They're going back on the milk with the bad weather and not being let in on the crofts."

Herd the cows! Not on his life! Jim was there one moment

and gone the next and Finlay might shout as loud as he liked, no one answered. "That boy! he'll come to a bad end," was Finlay's verdict. Jim, meanwhile, was on the bank of the river, throwing stones across. He'd go to Brae, yes! that's what he would do. Yet still he hesitated in an agony of indecision. Just then Alec John came in sight, whistling on a grass blade held between his two thumbs. Alec John, twelve years old, was the youngest son of Hugh Macdonald, the Bruces' right-hand neighbour. He was small for his age, tow-headed, and his ears stuck out like jug handles. "I can do it!" he said to Jim. "Watch this!" and he blew and he blew but nothing happened. Jim was just about to jeer at him when a different idea struck him.

"It's kind of stuffy down here," he said. "Let's climb up the hill a bit."

Alec John agreed and they climbed up the steep hillside, struggling through the long grass, panting and puffing, sometimes falling into tiny streams hidden by ferns and bracken, sometimes skirting an outcrop of rock till they gained the ridge and saw level ground ahead stretching away into the mist.

"Oof! Let's sit down," said Alec John. "Oh! look, Jim, how small the houses are from here." Jim nodded, quite amazed. The crofts looked about as big as handkerchiefs. The loch lay motionless as if it were made of glass, not water. Cloud hung on the hilltops.

"Let's keep along the ridge," Jim said, "then if the mist gets worse we can always follow a burn down the hill." Even up there the grass grew long and thick, having been free of nibbling sheep for a whole summer.

"Goodness! there's some grazing for cattle here," said Alec John. "My Dad says it's a shame putting sheep off a good hill like this one and all to grow a few logs." Jim had heard this view often enough at home, but he had also heard Murdo say that the wages the Forestry paid were a great help when there were poor prices for sheep and cattle. He didn't know who was in the right but Hugh, Alec John's father, was always laying off about something or other. He had stopped working when his family grew up, all except Alec John, and now he had all day for reading the paper and arguing.

The mist till then had lain ahead of them, now it slipped past eerily, touching their faces with its cold, clammy fingers, dampening their hair. Only a minute ago they had been safely outside it, now it enclosed them on all sides. The boys stopped walking, uncertain what to do.

" We might go over a waterfall," whispered Alec John.

" We'll sit down," said Jim, " then we can't come to any harm."

It was very quiet. They were cut off from the everyday world by these moving walls of cloud, this vast, silent dampness.

" What's that?" muttered Alec John.

" What?" whispered the other.

" Listen! Don't you hear it? Oh!——" Alec John sprang to his feet, as a huge animal loomed out of the mist, its horns like the branches of an oak. For seconds they gazed, rooted to the spot when suddenly Jim burst out laughing. " It's the white cow," he chortled, " and, oh! gosh, Alec, she's not big, she's wee!"

The little white cow stood looking at them, as much surprised as they were. She sniffed the air through her little black nostrils and then, giving a snort, moved away uphill with two big bullocks in her train.

" *They* looked as big as elephants," said Alec John, referring to the bullocks.

" It must be the mist," said Jim. " I didn't know it did that. Let's go on a bit, I'm getting cold. We should be near the end of the flat now."

" Don't let's fall over." They went on slowly till quite suddenly the mist lifted and they found themselves looking over to Brae which lay like the promised land, basking in sunshine.

" Oh! cheers!" cried Jim. " Come on, Alec John, we'll go and tell Alasdair his beasts are up here." The two boys went bounding down the hillside, glad to be clear of the eerie, clinging mist.

Alasdair was busy making dinner, keeping at the same time a weather eye on his cattle. Every now and then he went out and examined the hillside as far as he could see, almost to the head of the loch. During one of these inspections he caught sight of the boys and watched them till he was sure they were heading his way. Then he went in to stir the stew in the pot, wondering whether there would be enough for three, particularly if Jim proved to be one of the party for he had some idea of his appetite. There was no way of increasing the stew but he added another six potatoes to those already cooking. By that time the dogs were pricking up their ears and beginning to growl deep in their throats. When Alasdair went out the boys were out of sight, hidden by the green banks along the shore, but he could hear their voices. Quite soon their heads appeared at the top of the brae.

" Well! Well!" said Alasdair as he shook hands with them. "I was saying to myself it would be Jim and Tom coming to see how I was getting along, and I was half right and half wrong." He gave Alec John a keen glance. Jim told him who he was.

" Alec John, is it?" repeated Alasdair. "You'll be Hugh Macdonald's son, then. Och! I met your father and mother and the brother who works in the Forestry. Ewen, isn't he? And where have you been? I saw you coming down the slope yonder."

Having something to relate gave the boys the use of their tongues and between them they described their adventures on the top in the mist and how the wee cow had suddenly come upon them.

"Oh! is that where her ladyship is? I was wondering where

she'd got to. But I needn't have worried, for she's found a grand place for herself and she'll get the good of the grass before the frost cuts it."

"It was nearly up to our knees," said Alec John, still astonished.

Alasdair nodded. "The other bullocks—now, what were they like?"

But this stumped the boys, they hadn't really noticed anything except that they were black.

"Och! well, you wouldn't take particular notice," said Alasdair, a little regretfully, "but what am I thinking about, keeping you talking out here! Come away in." So saying Alasdair led the way into the house.

There had been big changes since the evening of the flitting. Shelves had been put up for dishes, the floor had been cleared, a sack filled with wool served as a cushion in a chair made out of a barrel. On a string nailed across one corner hung a towel, a pair of waterproof leggings, and two pairs of stockings.

"Well, what do you think of it now, Jim?"

"It's grand," said Jim.

"Well, it's not bad," replied Alasdair modestly, "and I hadn't much time for housekeeping either for the cattle keep me on the go. When they get on to the path they go on a route march and it takes me all my time if I don't notice them at once to catch up with them before they reach the drains. I promised the Forestry Commission when I came here that I'd keep the brutes from spoiling their drains and when you make a promise, Jim, you must keep it."

Jim nodded solemnly in agreement. "Well, now, I'm a wee bit short of chairs but you wait." So saying Alasdair plunged into the back room and came out with a fish box which, when put on its side, made a seat for both boys. He then stirred the stew and Jim sniffed the beautiful smell coming from the pot. "I've got the best larder in the countryside," Alasdair went on, chatting away to put his visitors at their ease, " and I'll show you where it is."

He went to the front door and pointed under the house—it was raised up on beams—" I'm sure you haven't a larder as good as that at your homes!"

" Do rabbits go in there? " asked Alec John.

" I'm telling you they do! They were popping in and out there the first few days till I felt I hadn't any business to be getting in the way but I doubt the dogs have scared them away since then, and that's a pity, for now I'll have to go for my dinner to the top of the hill. Do you like rabbit? Good! for there's some folk that can't abide it. Well, the potatoes are ready, boys, so if you're hungry we'll just sit down to it. You'll have to take things as you find them." After much searching Alasdair produced three knives but only two forks. " Och! well," he remarked philosophically, " it was fingers before forks."

The boys weren't fussy and soon had polished off a large plateful of rabbit stew, mopping up the gravy with the potatoes.

" That wasn't a bad stew," said Alasdair critically, " but there was just one thing wrong with it, it needed an onion for a bit of flavour but I haven't got one. See if you can find a biscuit in one of these boxes, Jim, and we'll finish off with a cup of tea." Jim tried all the boxes and found three large cabin biscuits in the last one. Butter and jam put on thickly made them quite good.

When the feast was over Alasdair sat down by the fire to smoke leaving the boys to do the washing-up. Jim had never washed a dish in his life since dish-washing was Sarah's province, but as there were no women in Brae he did what he was told with a good will, washing the plates and cups in a tin basin with what water was left over from tea-making. Alec John dried them on the towel.

" Well, boys, when I've had my smoke, what do you say to taking a walk up to the top, here, and you can see the rest of the cattle? " The boys were eager to explore farther but when

Alasdair got to his feet and was looking for his stick Jim happened to look out of the window and saw that some of the cattle beside the loch were beginning to move off in single file.

"I think they're going off," he said to his host.

Alasdair took a look. "The beggars!" he exclaimed. "They're off! We'll have to be after them, boys, for once they take the road they won't stop though there's grass up to their ears on both sides of them."

Off they set, the two dogs in their usual positions, Glen at heel and Spot a little way ahead. Alasdair's walk had a deceptively slow appearance but the boys soon found that they were always falling behind and that, to keep up with him, they had to run for short spells. The point was that the drover's pace never varied whether the ground was flat or whether the path rose as it did at times steeply. The boys were sweating even before they had circled the bay and reached the straight stretch of path which ran to the head of the loch. From the Brae cottage it was, of course, easy to see the whole face of Grasco, but now that they were themselves on it they could only see the short stretch of path ahead of them as it wound along and there was no sign of the animals.

"But as soon as we see them," Alasdair explained, "I can send Glen after them and save our own legs." Shortly afterwards they caught sight of the rear guard. "Away off!" Alasdair said to Glen and the dog leaped away, climbing above the cattle to come round them on the far side.

"Will he bring them all back?" asked Jim. Alasdair nodded and they stood waiting. Presently they heard the thud of the cattle's hoofs as they came racing back towards them with Glen at their heels. But this did not please Alasdair at all. "Take it easy, man!" he rebuked the dog who at once sank down, his eyes on his master, who stood counting the beasts as they filed past.

"Twelve! I doubt there was more than that. What do you think, boys?" They really had no idea but Jim risked saying that he was sure there had been more.

"Aye, well, we'll just take a turn to the next corner. It would be a pity to go back and leave some behind us."

Sure enough, standing in the bed of a small stream were three dun-coloured beasts.

"What do you mean?" inquired Alasdair of Glen as if he had been a human being. "What do you mean? Is that the way to behave yourself? I'm surprised at you." Glen looked thoroughly ashamed of himself but worse was to befall him as Alasdair sent Spot to repair his errors. He and Spot were rivals for their master's favour and had no love for each other. Spot was just bringing the three bullocks out of the burn when two women appeared and one of them drew back frightened.

Seeing this Alasdair hurried forward, saying, "Don't be afraid—the beasts will not harm you."

Mrs. Grant, the forester's wife, said that she was thankful to see him. "Those beasts of yours scare me out of my senses and all Charlie does is to laugh!"

Alasdair looked properly concerned. "Och! I'm sorry to hear that, Mrs. Grant. You don't need to worry about the beasts, for they're the quietest cattle you could meet in a day's march."

This made Mrs. Grant laugh heartily. "I'm *not* going on a day's march to prove it true! I've come too far as it is, but Ina is just like you and says there's nothing to worry about. Oh! I was forgetting—I don't believe you've met each other, though I think you know everyone else in the place."

"Pleased to meet you," said Alasdair and rung the teacher's hand till she winced. "You'll be used to cattle, I expect."

"Yes, I've lived among them all my life." They began discussing people they both knew. Alasdair had met her father at the Stirling sales and knew one of her brothers by sight. While this was going on the two boys moved away. All that talk! Not about anything interesting, only about people! Why, thought Jim resentfully, did *he* go on talking to her as if she was nice which she wasn't? Mrs. Grant said that they must be turning back and his heart rose only to fall again when Alasdair persuaded them to go a little way with him so that he could show them more cattle.

"That's for you, Ina." Mrs. Grant laughed. "For I'm sure I don't know one end of a beast from the other except for the horns."

"Dad was a good judge," Ina said in her off-hand manner, "but I'm not, still we can go a little farther." Alasdair turned to wave to the boys but they had disappeared.

"Her!" growled Jim. "What's she got to come along for? Pleased to meet her, was he? Ugh! Who'd be pleased to meet *her*, not if he knew what she was like anyway."

"Well, he can't know that because he never saw her before," said Alec John.

"Then he shouldn't say he was pleased!" retorted Jim. Green-eyed jealousy had him in her grip. Fancy Alasdair asking *her* to see the cattle! Cattle were for men to judge, not for women.

Alec John, in his heart of hearts, thought that Miss Menzies wasn't all that bad. If you knew your lessons—but, of course, Jim never knew his. He stayed silent, however, as he had no wish for Jim to start laughing and mocking at him.

The two boys loitered along the wayside, Jim accompanying Alec John to his house. He was never in a hurry to go home. He remembered the time when Sarah had taken him every Sunday afternoon to the old graveyard at the far end of the township. It was so old that some believed St. Columba's monks had been buried there close to the sea and there had been a little chapel. Sarah, dressed in her best clothes, a black hat on her head, and gloves on her work-chapped hands, used to move from one broken and tumbled down headstone to another, touching the moss and lichen, fingering the time-worn lettering, sighing as she skirted the tall nettles, burrs clinging to her skirt. Jim had whimpered when the nettles stung his legs but she had paid no attention, towing him after her on her erratic course from grave to grave. He had hated these weekly outings more almost than anything else in his drab life. Human warmth and kindness were not for him; he was alone, cut off with a person he feared. At last one Sunday he ran away just before she was ready to set off. When he was not to be found she had gone alone nor had she said anything to him. He had felt an immense relief.

As he kicked stones on the road and made an occasional remark to Alec John to keep him from going into his house he wondered why Sarah behaved in this way and when Alec John said, "Your mother's coming," Jim asked him if he knew.

"I dunno," Alec John replied, "she just always has. Mum says she's queer, that's why." Jim nodded and made for home. He didn't want to walk with Sarah. He found both men snoring, Finlay on the settle and Donald in the rocking chair. As soon as Sarah came in they both sat up though she had said nothing.

"Huh! you're back!" said her husband.

"Is it raining?" asked Finlay.

"That graveyard!" exlaimed Sarah, slowly peeling off one black cotton glove. "If you saw the graveyards down south! Beautiful, they were, just beautiful, with marble headstones and flowers under glass jars. I used to walk in them every Sunday." As she was taking the pin out of her rusty black hat she noticed Jim.

"So you're home, are you? Wanting your dinner, no doubt?"

"I am not," said Jim, but no sooner were the words spoken than he regretted them for Sarah leant towards him, her dark eyes set deep in their sockets, gazing hard at him. "And where did you get your dinner to-day, my bold lad?"

Warning bells rang in Jim's head. "I didn't have any dinner," he muttered. "I've a sore head."

She stayed quite silent, her eyes fixed on him till he wriggled uncomfortably. Then she spoke. "Telling lies as usual, Jim Smith, but it's not worth your while, for Mother will find out just where you've been." Deepening her tone, she continued, "You should love your mother, Jim, for she brought you up and did everything for you. No one would bother with you, you were such a puny little thing till I took care of you. Then tell your mother that you love her."

The words stuck in Jim's throat. She wasn't his mother, she had no right to use the word to him! But she came nearer, repeating her command. Still he could not reply. She asked a third time. Donald got out of his chair, Finlay put his feet on the floor.

"Yes!" he said, desperately. "Yes!"

"Yes what?"

"I love you," he muttered.

After a long moment she turned away. Finlay shuffled to the door, Donald kicked the dog out of his way, and Jim stayed slumped in his corner. He told many lies without a twinge of conscience but that was one lie which he hated telling.

5. Playing Truant

Now that Jim knew he was welcome at Brae he went as often as he possibly could. There was so much to see and do. Very soon it was as if he had been engaged as a herd boy and Alasdair was not satisfied till he knew every beast in the herd and could give an exact account of every animal he met on the track coming up. Well, of course, the highland cattle were easy to know apart. They varied in colour from yellow to bronze and reddish rust and over and above *that* their horns were a help for they, too, varied and once he had noted their exact shape he was sure of a beast ever after and could pick it out from a crowd. The same could be said of the cross-highland cattle but the Aberdeen Angus were the puzzlers. They were all black, they had no horns, so the only difference lay in their size and only too often they all seemed to be about the same size and weight. Jim found himself wrong time and again. He would report that he had seen the two bullocks from Staffin down at the Corry Mor burn only to be told that, no, he couldn't have for those two were away on the cliffs. Often enough he felt that it was no use, he'd never learn, but Alasdair wasn't too hard on him in those early days and would tell him to watch which beasts kept company together. "It'll come to you," he would say. "It'll come to you. Look at them, boy, look at them and then you can't go wrong!"

When they had leisure he told the boy stories of cattle sales, from the small outdoor variety in North Uist where the crofters kept grand cattle on the "machair," to the great mainland cattle marts of Dingwall, Perth, Inverness, and Stirling. He had once walked cattle from Skye to Fort William, crossing the narrows at Kylerhea to Glenelg and following the beasts slowly at two miles an hour up Mam Ratagan letting them feed by the way-side so that they were neither tired nor hungry. He had slept out in the heather, waking in the morning to the sound of the larks and the quiet breathing of the cattle all round. Jim would sit, hands clasped round his knees, brown eyes fixed on Alasdair's face, drinking in story after story of buying and selling, the profits he had made one hectic autumn when prices rose and rose, the losses which had followed when all of a sudden the market had collapsed.

"Och! you've got to take the rough with the smooth in droving," Alasdair always ended by saying. "It's fine to be making money but it's better still if you can smile when you're losing and you haven't as much money left as will buy a postage stamp."

One morning Jim had found Alasdair down on the rocks at low tide pulling a small seaweed off the rocks. "I've got a sick beast," he explained, "and this is an old cure. We'll boil this on the fire, pour off the liquid, and give it to her when it cools. Find bits of wood, Jim, lad, for we'll have a job making a huge pot boil on peats alone." Jim scoured the beach for driftwood and Alasdair kept poking little bits under the pot where it swung on the hook in the chimney. At last it boiled and just as well for all the wood had been used up. The peats kept it simmering. There was no cooked dinner that day for the big pot took the whole of the fire but they made do on bread and cheese. Alasdair was in a fever to be off but the water took a long time to cool even outside. Jim was sent out to search for bottles and was lucky to find a few on the lintel of the byre wall. They were covered in cobwebs and Alasdair, giving them one look, said, "Go and wash them." Jim took them to the burn, filled and refilled them with running water till at last they smelt sweet. Alasdair filled them with the brown liquid, and as there were no corks, put rolled-up paper in the necks of the bottles and told Jim to carry his carefully.

The heifer was standing alone, her head drooping, her sides hollow. Alasdair caught her, opened her jaws and showed Jim how to put the neck of the bottle on the top of her tongue and how to pour slowly so that she could swallow. They gave her two bottles of medicine in this way. Jim was thankful when the drover said that was enough at a time. "But we'll give her another dose to-morrow, Jim, as soon as you come up. Be as early as you can."

So it went on. There was always some way in which Jim could help and Jim never let on that he was playing truant from school.

He hadn't meant to in the first place, it had just happened. There had been a storm. The wind had risen in the night to gale force and veered to the worst quarter for Udale, namely the north-west. At one moment there was a flat calm and the next a squall hit the place like a tornado, slicing haystacks in two, flinging stooks of corn into the air, covering the fences with flying hay. After a three-months' struggle with bad weather the crofters were back almost where they had begun. Jim was kept off school for two days to help salvage what they could once the rain had ceased and the wind had dried the soaked ground.

On the second day Alasdair had arrived to meet the van at the Bruces' house but it was late, held up by the weather and he couldn't wait. "I've a beast missing," he told Sarah, " and I'll need to go right back, so I'll give you a line (he meant a list of what he wanted) and the money and, perhaps, if you get through the work Jim could come up with it in the evening."

"But I told him," Sarah recounted with glee, " that Jim had no time, we'd be working all day, he'd just have to come himself."

" He thinks nobody has anything to do but wait on him,"
growled Finlay, " and him without a care in the world."

Jim fumed and fretted inwardly. Why couldn't his foster-
parents give a neighbour a helping hand? To do so never
harmed anyone. He planned to slip off at dusk but when the
time came he was too scared of the dark. Being tired after a
long day's work he slept at once. But all of a sudden he woke
just as if someone had poked him in the ribs. The room was
dark, Finlay was breathing heavily beside him. Why had he
wakened as if obeying an order? Then he remembered the bag
on the dresser. They'd send him to school that day and Alasdair
would have to fetch his own groceries. He wouldn't think
much of Jim, he'd say he was tarred with the same brush as the
Bruces, never willing to offer a helping hand. All at once he
knew what he must do. He'd get up at once—he didn't know the
time but it must be early—go to Brae before breakfast, and then
straight on to school. Very, very cautiously he crawled to the
foot of the bed where only Finlay's feet lay between him and the
door. He stepped gingerly over them, the bed creaked, and
Finlay tossed over, grunting, " Eh?" Jim froze. Seconds as long
as hours passed. Then the rhythm of Finlay's snores began again.

Carrying his trousers, socks, and boots, Jim reached the
kitchen and was putting one leg into his trousers when something rubbed against the other.

The hair at the back of his head rose and he shivered violently
before realising that it was only Sarah's cat. He shoved it away,
angry because it had given him such a fright. He took the rucksack, tiptoed into the scullery, and searched for the oil can for
the back door key squeaked badly. With a feather from the
drawer he oiled the lock freely, then pushed the oil can out of
sight and turned the key. Without a sound Jim stepped out into
the early morning air but as he shut the door Ben, the old dog,
barked from his shed. Jim hushed him as he passed, then took a
look at the hens' laying boxes and saw two eggs. Just the job!

With them in his pocket he took the road to Brae. It was not quite dark, for a faint light gleamed from the loch and from the sky, enough to show him his way. He went along at a half trot, so delighted with his successful escape that walking was too tame for him. He was soon past the forester's house and when he

came abreast of the sea noticed that the tide was on the ebb. That was lucky because he would be able to cross over the beach on his way back and so avoid being seen from home. One solitary light shone across the water. He guessed that it came from the schoolroom which Murdo's wife cleaned every morning. The sky behind Ben Mor was growing steadily lighter and just as he reached the fork in the path the sun rose over its shoulder. Brae was still in shadow but behind him Udale shone in the sun. Every bush, every blade of grass even, looked as if it had just been made for him alone. What a glorious feeling to be out and about so early when nearly everyone else was frowsting in bed! With a bit of luck he might even find Alasdair still sleeping! He hurried on but as he crossed the plank over the Corry Mor burn he saw the first smoke from the cottage chimney spiralling thickly upwards into the still air. The smell of peat reached him as he hastened along the shore. Alasdair came out for a pail of water as Jim panted his way up the last slope to receive a warm welcome.

" Why, Jim, my hero, is this you already! You're a welcome sight for I'm out of tobacco and a lot of other things besides, but I believe I could do without the rest if I had the baccy. Terrible how it takes a hold of a man." So saying, he emptied the contents of the rucksack to make certain the tobacco was really there. Jim, for his part, had an eye on a pound of bacon.

" You'll be hungry? " That was a question which didn't need asking. Jim, having run most of the way, was starving. The smell of the bacon on the frying pan made his mouth water. " We could do with an egg," Alasdair remarked, " but we'll just have to do without." At this Jim produced two eggs from his pocket and wonder of wonders, they were both whole.

" Jim! you're a friend in need. Och! now, that was very kind of your mother. Eggs are scarce at this time of the year. Thank her kindly from me and we'll have to see if we can catch a rabbit for her." Alasdair was busy spooning fat over the eggs and didn't see Jim's flush of dismay. " Put the table to rights, boy! "

" There isn't a table! " Jim laughed.

" Och! well, you know what I mean—the tea chest. I've been meaning to make myself a table for weeks for there's plenty of driftwood that would do fine but what with these beasts thinking they're Derby racers and others falling sick or going lost I just haven't a minute."

" Did you find the one that was lost yesterday? "

Alasdair nodded as he dished up the bacon and egg. " Aye! I

did but he took a few miles out of my legs before I spotted him. Now tuck in, boy."

Jim thought it the best breakfast he had ever tasted. The sun was shining on the sparkling loch, the sky was blue, and the whole world was in holiday mood. When Alasdair had eaten he sat down to look at a whole week of newspapers which had come at one time so Jim tidied up and when he had finished he stood by the window, saying to himself, " I'd better be off, I've still time to make it," when Alasdair, glancing up from his paper, said, " If you're not in a hurry, Jim, we can go up and look at the snares. I got three yesterday. Of course, if they're needing you——"

" They don't need me—we finished the stacking yesterday," said Jim and never mentioned school. The day passed all too quickly. They found two rabbits in snares and Alasdair wanted Jim to take them but Jim said that the Bruces hated rabbits. " Aye, well, is that so? We'll need to think of something else, then." They took a turn round the cattle reaching over what Alasdair termed " the back." Ahead of them Jim could see the land rise to the great headlands facing the Minch.

" Seven miles of coast and most of it cliff! " commented Alasdair. " I'll lose a few over the rocks before the year is out." He shaded his eyes to examine the skyline and shook his head. " Just what I was afraid of! There they are right back on the top with a three hundred foot drop below them. I drove them away only yesterday." He hesitated and then shrugged. " I'm as well to leave them as they are. If I move them they come charging back and it's then they're apt to push each other over. It's a risk I'll have to take."

All too soon Jim had to say it was time for him to go. He aimed to arrive home as if coming from school. Alasdair gave him final instructions about the cattle on Grasco, he was to turn their heads homeward and move them off the path. He stood watching the boy grow small in the distance. The lad had taken a right fancy to him and for all his backwardness he had the makings of a good cattleman. Alasdair smiled a little to himself as he climbed the steps of the house. He knew he had a way with people, especially young people. He had always been able to get all the help he wanted, no matter where he was. Now, his brother, Norman, was a great one for working away all day long every day of the year. For all that, he, Alasdair, could make more at one sheep sale than Norman could in a whole year with all his hard work.

The men were having dinner, Sarah waiting on them as she always did, when Jim reached home. He was met by a barrage of questions. Why had he gone off in the morning without his breakfast? Where had he been? Where had the rucksack gone to? Jim answered quickly that he had seen Alasdair coming and had given it to him. Where had he been? He'd been at school, of course, he had gone early to get the homework from Tom for the teacher was cross if you didn't know your lessons. This zeal for doing homework was something new and all three stared at him but before they could express disbelief Jim hurried on, " *She* says you're to send a line the next time you keep me off, she says she wants a line every time."

The stratagem worked better than Jim had hoped. " A line!" exclaimed Sarah in her deep contralto. " She wants a line! Well she knows why we kept you! There's no need for a line for the like of that!"

" Wasn't she born on a croft herself?" grunted Donald. " She knows very well why you were kept off with the hay and the corn scattered to the four winds."

" Obh! Obh! Obh!" cried Finlay. " Some people are getting too big for their boots." Jim was delighted. He had thrown them a bone to growl over for the rest of the evening and they didn't give him or his doings another thought.

" A line, indeed! And I remember when her uncle was on the Poor Law!"

" Wasn't every scholar in the school off? Were you the only one asked to bring a line? Is it to be one thing for us and something different for everyone else? "

Jim, sitting down to what remained of the dinner, explained smugly that everyone had to bring a line.

" She'll get no line from me! " said Sarah, and then after a few minutes' silence, " Line, indeed! "

Out fetching water from the well, Jim laughed and slapped his leg. Oh! he was a clever fellow, he was indeed! There was no one like him! He'd just go to Brae whenever he felt like it and no one would be a penny the wiser.

6. Punishment

The wind rattled the window sash. Miss Menzies put down the school register with a sigh as the door opened and Effie Mackenzie came in carrying the supper tray.

"I really don't know what to do," she said, frowning, "I just don't know what to do." Effie had no idea what all this was about but, having placed the tray on the table, she bent down to sweep up the hearth hoping to hear more. "It's that boy, Jim Smith, he's hardly ever in school nowadays."

Effie looked properly concerned but said nothing. Jim's behaviour had been discussed in the kitchen a few times, but, thought Effie, it may be all gossip.

Miss Menzies continued to look thoroughly annoyed. "Can it be work? Are they still at the harvest? You've finished, haven't you?"

"Oh! we've all finished, I think," replied Effie, "unless it's potatoes—we had a job lifting ours and there was a terrible smell off one corner of the field, so Murdo said we'd just leave it and I must say I wasn't sorry—they weren't fit for the hens let alone human beings."

Miss Menzies clicked her tongue. "Well, if it's not work, what is it? I've told him till my tongue is tired that he's to bring a note whenever he's absent but he says his mother won't write one. Do you think that could be true?"

Effie creased her brow in the effort to answer this question. "Well, indeed, I couldn't say. I know I'm often lazy enough myself because it means looking for a pen and then maybe the ink's dry and sometimes we run out of writing paper——" she paused uncertainly.

"Well, it's the law," said Miss Menzies, biting into a pancake well covered with butter and jam. "I suppose I must go and see his mother; we can't go on like this. The education sub-committee will start asking questions and then I'll get into trouble. Not that I want to see him in school. He's just a trouble-maker, whispering and making mischief at the back. I'll be glad when he leaves. I don't know, there's something about him—of course, we don't know where he came from."

"That's right," agreed Effie, "these adopted children—you just don't know how they'll turn out."

"Is he related, do you think, to the Bruces?"

"Well, now, nobody knows. Kursty Morag says he has a look of Sarah—she was a MacPhail—but I don't see it myself. Murdo says it was Donald's idea, that he wanted someone to do the work and they wouldn't need to pay him but I don't know. I remember fine—it was just about this time of year when Sarah went to Glasgow and brought him back with her. The first day he went to school—I mind it yet—our Tom brought him in here so that I could warm him up. He was a poor wee thing with those great brown eyes of his staring out of his thin little face."

"Your Tom is a treasure," said the teacher. "I'll be as sorry to lose him as I shall be glad to lose the other one."

Effie, back in the big kitchen, reported this conversation to her husband, who nodded his big head at her praise of Tom. "But don't be hard on the other lad, Effie, that's not like you."

"Well! Murdo," she flared up, "I'm tired of washing ink-stains out of Mary's clothes and mending tears in Donnie's jacket and it's your Jim Smith who throws the ink and your Jim Smith that spoils Donnie's clothes."

"Tom and him are great friends," said Murdo with aggra-vating mildness.

"It would take a very badhearted boy to quarrel with our Tom!" retorted Effie, rattling crockery in the sink, but presently her annoyance faded and she said, "Well, I don't mean he's so very bad, poor lad, perhaps if they were a bit kinder to him——" She left the sentence in mid-air but Murdo knew quite well what she meant.

The following afternoon Miss Menzies went to the Bruces' house. The fact was noted by every child on his way home from school and by most of the parents from the kitchen window or the byre doorway. "The boy will be in trouble now," was the verdict. Everyone knew, had known for some time, where he was, everyone, that is, except the Bruces. Sarah was all civility to the teacher who reminded her of the gentry she had served

in hotels in the good old days. She chased the cat off the best chair and insisted on Miss Menzies seating herself there though she would have preferred to stand or else to sit on the edge of a hard chair as easier to escape from. However, she sat down and then said abruptly because she was nervous, "I've come about your son, he's not been attending school regularly and he never brings a line to say why he's been absent."

Sarah began rocking herself backwards and forwards. " Oh! dear me, oh! dear me," she repeated over and over.

" Is he ill ? "

" No, no, he's never ill, a hardy boy."

" Then are you keeping him off to help on the croft ? " But Sarah went on rocking and didn't answer. Miss Menzies felt far from comfortable. This interview was becoming even more awkward than she had feared.

" Are you keeping him off for any reason, Mrs. Bruce ? If he's ill he must have a doctor's certificate, you know."

Sarah stared at her without answering. Miss Menzies tried again. " I'm afraid you must see that he comes to school. You do understand, don't you, that he's breaking the law. He can't leave school till he's fourteen."

" Breaking the law! Breaking the law! A terrible thing to break the law! "

The way the woman kept repeating her words gave Miss Menzies a most uneasy feeling. " Well, that's all right, then," she said, getting to her feet. " I'll expect Jim in school to-morrow."

" Beautiful," Sarah muttered, her eyes on her guest's hair which was wound in thick pleats round her head. " Beautiful! You're like the people I used to know, such nice clothes and such nice manners, not like this place, all rough and hard, no, no, not like this place." All Miss Menzies wanted was to get away as quickly as possible. She put her hand on the door handle but the woman stretched out her own hand which was rough as sandpaper and covered hers.

" So he is not going to school ? " she queried, peering at the schoolmistress in the gloom.

" No, he is not going." They stood like that for what seemed to the young woman an age, then at last Sarah drew back.

" He will go to school, Miss Menzies, you need not be afraid of that any more."

" Thank you," was all Miss Menzies could find to say. As she hurried to her own warm fireside she tried to shake off the curious impression the whole visit had made on her. At least, she thought, that's over, what am I worrying about ?

Jim had had one of his happiest days. He and Alasdair had done all sorts of things from bringing driftwood up above the tide mark to making a supply of pins for rabbit snares. Best of all he had come out of a test set him by Alasdair with a fair amount of credit. Alasdair had gone part of the way home with him and just as they were parting they came on a group of Aberdeen-Angus bullocks. " Pick the best out of that lot," said Alasdair. Jim studied the animals from the front, the side, and the rear. " There's not much between them," he said to gain time—his heart was beating fast as he longed to show that he had benefited from Alasdair's lessons. Alasdair grunted—nothing to be learnt from that; there was nothing for it but to chance his luck, but first he circled them once more then, " That one !" He pointed, but Alasdair shook his head.

" No, this one here, he's got a deeper chest. He's not in as good condition as yours but you wait till you see him in the summer. Oh! you didn't make a bad choice at all. I'd have put yours second myself. You're learning, you're learning." Almost bursting with pride, Jim hurried on his way. It was already growing dark. He had been growing more and more careless, not even bothering to arrive home as if just out of school. He kept making up excuses—he had been playing football with the boys or had run a message for a neighbour. But now a small chill of apprehension touched him. It *was* late. No one could be playing football to this hour. What could he say to Sarah? He broke into a run.

At home Sarah was looking at the clock, her father's old clock, which hung on the wall, the pendulum swinging from side to side. "A quarter past six," she said.

Donald stirred in his seat by the fire. "That clock's fast."

Sarah picked up the alarm clock on the dresser—it would only go with its face to the wall—"Twenty past six!" she announced triumphantly. "So where is my fine fellow now?" Donald's only answer was a grunt, but Finlay echoed, "Aye, where is he?" Then Jim walked in. Silence, but he felt three pairs of eyes staring at him. Gosh! there was something far wrong. Mind your step, Jim Smith. He sat down. Still the silence was unbroken. It was more unnerving than a whole chorus of shouts. Ben pushed his heavy head on to his knee and Jim tickled him behind the ears. Relief came from the most unlikely quarter. "Where have you been?" cried Finlay in his high, squeaky voice. Better to have the row start and get it over and done with.

"I was playing with the boys," he muttered, looking at the floor.

"Lift your head, Jim Smith, and say that to me again."

He looked reluctantly at Sarah. "I was playing with the boys."

Sarah's glance shifted to her husband. "You see?" was all she said but a shiver went through the boy. They were on to something this time. What could he do? Almost against his will he began elaborating the story. They had been playing near the river, someone had kicked the ball into the bushes or into the river, they couldn't make out which because it was getting so dark. "It was Donnie's ball," he ended. Sarah's unnatural calm broke. "You see," she shrieked. "Lies! Lies! Lies! What do we ever get from him but lies? The ones who feed him and are good to him—lies! lies!"

Her words acted on Donald like a spur to a horse. He jumped to his feet.

"You tell the truth for once. What have you been up to?"

"Where have you been all day?" came from Finlay.

"I was at the school," repeated Jim desperately, no longer believing the lie would do him any good but unable to think of anything else.

"You were at the school, were you?" Donald repeated after a nerve-racking pause. "It's a queer thing you always come back from school by the Brae road?"

"I—I—cr-cross over the river." The words were hard to get out.

"That's enough of that!" exclaimed Donald, past patience. "You've been up at Brae, that's the school you've been at."

He loosened his belt.

Sweat broke out on Jim. "I'll go to school to-morrow!" he said, his mouth dry.

"You will indeed," replied Donald, "though maybe you won't be able to sit down." He bared his broken teeth in a grin more frightening than a curse.

"Don't hit me! Don't hit me!" the boy begged, and even as he begged he was ashamed of himself. Of course, they would hit him. There was no hope. The belt came down, he yelled, struggled in Finlay's grasp, kicked, and writhed, the dog howled under the table and Sarah shrieked over and over, "Punish him, Donald, punish him, punish him." At last it was over. They flung him into the little back room. They banged the door shut. Old Ben howled once more and was kicked.

"Take the dog out to the shed!" Donald snarled. Finlay shuffled off with him.

Sarah sat rocking by the fire. " Oh! the disgrace," she murmured. " Breaking the law! I can't hold up my head."

" He'll not do it again in a hurry. Make the tea, wife."

Two hours later Finlay went into the room for an ounce of tobacco. His best suit was on the back of a chair beneath the wide open window. The suit was soaking wet and the room was empty.

7. The Search

"Jim Smith. Jim Smith!" Miss Menzies looked up from the register next day and frowned on her pupils. "Has anyone seen Jim Smith?"

There was a chorus of "No, Miss." Miss Menzies tightened her lips, closed the register, and put it back in her desk. This was really too much! This was going beyond the limit! The children noted the storm signals and nudged each other. One thing was certain—Jim would catch it when he did turn up.

Over in Grasco Murdo Mackenzie was standing outside the forestry shed with his mare in the cart beside him and wishing he'd never harnessed her that morning, but there had been a break in the clouds making him think the weather was going to improve. The wind had backed, however, sou'westerly and now the rain was worse than ever. The forestry workers were playing cards on a packing case inside the shed.

"Heh! Ewen," Murdo shouted. "I'm away home—it's on for the day."

Ewen poked his head outside the door. "Aye! you're right, Murdo, we'll tell Grant." Murdo led the mare back round the road. Once they had crossed the bridge they were head-on into the wind. The mare was jittery, the least unexpected noise startling her, even the flapping of Murdo's oilskin.

"It's all right, old girl," Murdo said consolingly, "We'll soon have you back in your stable." The words were scarcely out of his mouth when two figures leapt across the road to confront him. The mare's ears went back flat to her head, the next

75

moment she was up on her hind legs with Murdo, all sixteen stone of him, hanging on to her mouth for dear life.

For any favour! There was Donald Bruce waving his stick right ahead of him and with the tail of his eye Murdo caught sight of Finlay looking equally threatening just behind him. What in the world was up? The mare came down on all four feet and did her best to bolt.

"Easy does it, Sally, take it easy, lass," Murdo implored her. "Go easy with that stick, Donald, you know Sally is a bit nervous."

"Where's the boy?" was all Donald said.

"What boy?"

"Fine you know what boy I mean. Don't try being clever with me, Murdo Mackenzie! Where's the boy?" Donald's voice had risen to a shout and over and above the shriek of the wind Murdo caught Finlay's echo, "Where's the boy?"

"Whoa! there, lass, gently, now, we'll soon be home," Murdo said coaxingly to the mare who was still showing the whites of her eyes, and then to Donald, "If you mean your own boy, I don't know where he is, I haven't seen him. Is he not in the school?"

"You know well he's not in the school!" Donald glowered even more darkly, for he thought Murdo was laughing at him. "He hasn't been in the school all week."

"I haven't seen your Jim, Donald, since goodness knows when. I'll ask Tom, he might know. When did you miss him?" At that, to Murdo's surprise, they fell back a little and muttered to each other. Seizing the chance Murdo urged the mare on. Sally was only too pleased and very soon they had left the Bruces far behind.

Miss Menzies was in the Lodge kitchen for a mid-morning cup of tea. "If that doesn't beat the band," she was saying. "His mother *promised* he'd be at school to-day and *now* what can I do?"

"Indeed, I thought they'd be sure to send him to-day after you going all that way yesterday," said Effie, warming the tea-pot. Just then Murdo came in, water running off his oilskins. "Oh! goodness, Murdo, I didn't know the rain was so bad."

"I had to come back," explained Murdo, wiping his face on the towel his wife gave him. "I had a job getting home at all," he added.

"How do you mean, Murdo? Is the river in flood?"

"Oh, no, it wasn't that." Murdo told the two women what had happened and added, "It only wanted Sarah to come running after me with her black petticoats flapping in the gale, for me and Sally to land up in the loch. She nearly pulled my arm out of the socket."

"Oh! Murdo," cried Effie in an immediate agitation. "I've been telling you for years the mare's not safe."

"There's nothing wrong with the mare!" retorted Murdo, as near to sharpness as he ever went. "It's what's wrong with the Bruces, that's the point to my mind. Sally wasn't minding the wind and rain till they came along——"

But Miss Menzies wasn't interested in Sally's character at that moment. "But where is Jim?" she asked. "Surely that's the point."

"Where, indeed?" repeated Effie. "It's no day for being outside."

"If you ask me," said Murdo, warming his hands on a mug of scalding tea, "it's up in Brae he is."

"Is *that* where he's been going? Yes, of course, I might have known it, it's since MacAskill came to the place that Jim's been playing truant. Well, really, it's too bad!"

"Maybe Alasdair doesn't know Jim's still at school," suggested Murdo, but the teacher pooh-poohed this idea.

"He's just making use of him," she said. "They say he's very selfish for all his charm—if you call it charm. Thinks of nobody but himself."

But Effie did not like to hear Alasdair miscalled. "He's got a very kind heart," she said. "But, Murdo, why should the Bruces think we had Jim?"

"That's the puzzle," agreed her husband. "We've mouths enough of our own to feed without adding another! Och! you know the Bruces, Effie, they act first and think afterwards." Then quite suddenly he began to laugh and couldn't stop. The mug trembled so much in his hand that Effie was obliged to take it from him and place it on the table. "If you'd seen them!" he gasped. "One on each side of me, like a hold-up, Donald shouting and Finlay echoing every word and me pleading with Sally one moment and trying to reason with them the next. I might as well have reasoned with Sally—a sight better—oh! well, it was a laugh." And Murdo wiped his streaming eyes. But Effie was not amused. It was always a bad thing to fall out with a neighbour in a small place. Although the Bruces were difficult they had so far managed to live at peace with them. But this looked like the beginning of a feud. Although how even the Bruces could blame Murdo, Effie failed to understand.

By this time the Bruces were, in fact, blaming someone else. It stood to reason that if Murdo was not at fault then Alasdair MacAskill was. They had only to pronounce his name to become quite certain that he was the culprit. With one accord they set off in the opposite direction, crossed the bridge, and took the path to Brae. They were passing the forester's house when they saw the dogs, Glen and Spot, outside the door. The Bruces stopped dead in their tracks and looked at one another. They need go no farther.

Alasdair was indeed seated comfortably beside the fire, with his feet up, drying his stockings. He had had to dash after the cattle on one of their raids to the head of the loch. He, the forester, and the forester's wife, Charlotte, were all chatting away happily when they heard a bang on the back door. "Must be something wrong!" Charlie exclaimed, at once thinking of an accident to one of the men. But when he flung the door open he saw the two Bruces, one behind the other.

"Come in! Come in!" he said hospitably. Besides, the rain was driving straight into the back kitchen.

But the Bruces shook their heads. "We'll no' come in. We want Alasdair MacAskill." On hearing his name Alasdair swung his legs down and got to his feet.

"What's the matter, Donald?" he asked cheerfully. "Have you a beast sick?"

"No! I have not. Where's the boy?" Alasdair was so surprised by this unexpected question that he stammered like a guilty person. "If it's Jim you mean I saw him last night about four o'clock, no, no, it must have been after five. He was on his way home then. Do you mean he never reached?"

This question seemed to cause Donald some bother. He hummed and hawed as one caught out in his stride.

"Did he reach home?" Alasdair repeated, really anxious by this time and puzzled by the Bruces' curious behaviour. The boy might have tripped in the half dark and broken an ankle. Perhaps he was lying at that moment under the pelting rain! Alasdair took a step towards them, waiting their reply, and then a quick step back as the pool of rainwater near the door soaked through his stockings once again.

"He reached home," Donald said as if it were forced out of him.

"Will you not come in?" Charlotte Grant now added her voice to the general demand. There was a terrible draught with the back door open and she was afraid the baby would catch a cold.

"When did he leave, then?" Alasdair persisted. "When did you miss him?"

"Last night."

"Last *night*?" cried the forester, startled.

" Oh! the poor boy!" exclaimed Charlotte, quite forgetting about the draught. " It was a terrible night of rain."

" We'd better organise a search party," said Alasdair, a worried frown creasing his brow.

" Could he have gone up to Brae without you knowing, Alasdair?" Charlie Grant asked.

Alasdair shook his head. " I don't think so—I've just come along the path—unless he went clean off it in the dark. If he did he could easily be lying with a broken neck."

The Bruces cried out at this. " And if he is, it's your fault, Mr. MacAskill. We had no trouble with the boy till you came! You have been leading him astray. You will hear more about this—we are not finished with you, Mr. MacAskill."

It was the way they used his English name that showed how badly they were upset.

Alasdair was flabbergasted. " But I had no idea you didn't want him to come and see me. You never said a word to me——"

" Was the boy not at the school?" countered Donald furiously. " You'll not pretend you didn't know *that*?"

" At school? Jim at school?"

" That's where he should be but you are after spoiling him— but we will make you pay for this yet—don't you be a bit afraid—Mr. MacAskill." And with this parting shot they turned about and marched off, one behind the other, as they had come.

Mrs. Grant shut the door. " Well!" she said. " Oh! dear," and sat down on the nearest chair.

" They're upset," Charlie said, " but we must get a search party at once or he may die of exposure. Make some sandwiches, wife, and a flask."

" The dinner won't be long," his wife lamented. But he replied, " We've no time to waste. I'll get the men—lucky they're still in the shed. We'll make two parties, Alasdair."

" Aye! right, I'll get my boots on." And as he struggled to

get his feet into wet boots he said, " School! I hadn't the least idea——"

" Oh! Alasdair, you must have known!" said Mrs. Grant, hurrying to make sandwiches. " Surely you saw him over at the school some time?"

" I saw him once at the Lodge but I didn't know he was in *school*. He's that tall I thought he was over fourteen—sure as I'm here. If I'd known the first thing about it do you think I'd have let him miss the school?" He sounded most aggrieved. As Mrs. Grant saw the men coming she said no more. The search was on.

Later that day Tom was letting the byre cattle in. They filed past him, each going to his own stall. The water ran off their coats. They were glad to get into shelter. Tom went from one to the other slipping chains round their necks.

"Move over, Bess!" he ordered the brindled cow, for she had swung her rump against her neighbour and Tom couldn't squeeze between them. "Go on!" he repeated. "Move over." As he bent to pick up the chain a small stone hit him on the back. "Och! stop it, Donnie, don't try and be funny." When he had finished tying the cow he looked round but saw no one. No doubt Donnie was hiding in the next stall. Then he heard "Tom! Tom!" from above and knew who it was. He drew the outside doors together and then ran up the ladder to the loft.

"Jim?" he whispered. "Where are you?"

"Here!" Jim was lying curled in a nest he had made by lying in the hay all night. "Oh! Tom, I'm so hungry. I was waiting and waiting for you to come."

"Goodness! I never thought of you being here, Jim, honest I didn't. We thought you must be up in Brae."

"It was too dark—I couldn't go. Get me something to eat, Tom, I'm famished." Tom slid down the ladder. As soon as he left the byre the wind caught him, pushing him along. He ran across the yard, doubled up, and slipped into the scullery. He could hear voices in the kitchen so he opened the bread bin stealthily and saw the heel of a loaf and newly baked scones wrapped in a white cloth. He shoved the loaf under his jacket and was opening the cloth when Mary looked in.

"What are you doing, Tom? You can't be hungry already?"

"Can't I?" replied Tom tersely.

"Mummy! Mummy! Tom's eating scones and he's just had his dinner."

"If he's hungry, dear——" came Effie's voice from the kitchen. "Did you feed the cows?"

"I'm feeding them," Tom muttered.

"Feeding yourself, more like!" said Mary pertly.

"Don't forget the stirks in the shed," said his mother—as if he ever did! "And take some jam for your piece." With Mary's sharp eyes on him all Tom wanted was to escape. He had a very strange feeling as if he were doing something wrong and mustn't be found out.

Jim swallowed all he had brought him in less than no time. "Thanks, Tom, I could eat a whale. What's happening?"

"They're out searching for you, everyone."

Jim thought this funny but Tom felt far from happy. Suppose his father asked him if he had seen Jim what could he say? He didn't want to have to tell lies. Jim broke in on his thoughts with, "What will I do, Tom?"

"I don't know—why did you run away?"

"They beat me."

"They often beat you," Tom said, meaning that one beating more or less was no reason.

"They're not going to beat me any more," Jim replied fiercely. "I'm not going to stay. I don't know where I'll go but I'll go." There was a long silence while the rain drummed on the roof and the wind howled in the elms. Jim went on: "I can go to sea for a while till I'm older, I can earn money and then I'll come—come back and—and—buy cattle."

"Huh-huh! but how are you to get away? You can't go by road or they'll see you. Unless you could stow away in the *Seagull*?"

"Of course, that's the very thing," Jim burst in eagerly, forgetting to keep his voice low. "She often sails to Mallaig. I could slip off when they were buying stores——"

"Tom! Tom! Who are you talking to up there?" The two boys froze. They heard footsteps on the ladder. This galvanised Tom into action. He scrambled across the hay and got his feet on the top rung of the ladder just in time to prevent Donnie landing on the hay.

"What are you sitting there for? Let me up!"

"I'm coming down," was all Tom replied, suiting the action to the word, and as he was bigger and heavier than his brother, the latter had to climb down.

"I was seeing if there was a hen's nest up there," Tom went on, quite surprised at his own capacity to tell lies. "Mum says there's one or two laying yet and she's not getting the eggs."

"Did you get them?" Tom shook his head. He put his boot on the bottom rung and began to tie his lace.

"Let me up! I'll have a look, I'm better at finding things than you."

"No."

"Why shouldn't I look?"

"Dad says it's bad for the hay to be trampling all over it— the cows won't eat it."

"Och! away," retorted Donnie in a tone of disbelief. Tom took no notice, he was still tying his laces. Donnie waited. "They're both tied now," he said pointedly.

"Aye," replied Tom.

Donnie tried again. "Who were you talking to up there?"

"To myself."

"Are you going to be like Kursty Morag and talk to yourself?" Donnie scoffed.

Tom said nothing. It was nearly dark in the byre, the cows shifted their feet and rattled their chains, looking for the food which was slow in coming.

Suddenly, Donnie dashed out of the byre shouting, "I know who's up there! You can't fool me!"

"Donnie!" Tom called in a panic. "Donnie, come back!" But already the boy was out of sight. Still, Tom ran after him, reproaching himself that he hadn't told Donnie and trusted him not to tell. He had made a right mess! When he reached the house Donnie was already in the kitchen pouring out his story. Worse still the kitchen was full of people for one of the search parties had just that moment arrived.

" He's here! He's here! He's in the loft, Tom's talking to him."

" What? What's that you're saying?" Murdo's heavy hand caught his son by the arm.

" It's true, Dad, you don't need to hold me like that—*I'm* not telling lies." Murdo resisted an impulse to shake the boy. Instead he pushed him aside and strode out to the barn.

" Jim! Jim! " he called. " Come down, lad, we know you're there." But there was no answer. He called three times, then from outside came a sudden shout: " There he goes! "

Out across the fields towards the graveyard the boy was running. Close behind went his pursuers. They were gaining, they were spreading out, those nearest the sea getting ahead of the fugitive, prepared to cut him off. The boy dodged, making for the hill. " After him, Ewen! " The watchers strained their eyes in the dusk. The boy disappeared down the bank of a burn, Ewen at his heels. There could be only one end. Murdo turned abruptly and went into the house. Tom was standing looking miserable. " I'll speak to you later," Murdo said. " Go up to your room."

But Tom stood his ground though his voice trembled. " Dad! don't send him back."

" Be quiet! Now, go to your room. I didn't think *you* would tell me lies, Tom."

" I didn't—I haven't——" Tom began but there was no time for explanations. The search party came in dragging Jim with them. The chase had ended when he fell in the burn, cutting his right knee. Water poured off him.

" Well! you're a fine one," exclaimed the forester. " The whole place out looking for you and you lying snug in the hay! What on earth were you playing at? What got into you? "

" We thought we'd find you with a broken ankle at least! " Ewen Macdonald added. He had already given Jim a piece of his mind on their way back from the burn. He was such a miserable looking object, however, as he stood there, his clothes sticking to his thin body, his hair plastered to his head, and blood running in a channel through the dirt on his leg, that the searchers, cold, wet, and tired as they were, had not the heart to scold him any further.

" You'll have a cup of tea," said Effie, reaching for the teapot, but Charlie shook his head.

" We'd better be making tracks before we soak the kitchen," he said, " and we'll need to get in touch with the others—they're still out searching."

With a feeling of relief the search party moved in a body to the door.

Murdo ordered his wife to fetch him some of Tom's clothes and the rest of the family to go upstairs. He, himself, undressed Jim, took a towel from the pulley and rubbed him down from his wet hair to his feet, and bandaged his knee. He dressed him in Tom's clothes and then busied himself putting food on the table.

When he had made Jim a pot of tea he sat down himself, filled his pipe, and settled down for a quiet smoke.

But Jim ate nothing.

" Take the tea, boy, it'll do you good."

" I can't go back—I can't—I can't——" Jim broke out.

" It'll be all right," Murdo said in a matter-of-fact way. " You will see, it'll be all right."

" It won't, it won't," Jim answered. " They'll beat me again."

Murdo had seen the marks of that other beating on Jim's back but all he said was, " No! they won't beat you, I'll see to that."

" You won't be there! "

" I will be there," Murdo replied. " I'm going home with you and I'll talk to them. It'll be all right, Jim, lad, don't worry."

But the boy trembled and shook. "I want to get away," he muttered.

"You'll get away soon," Murdo said gently. "You're getting big now, you'll soon be leaving school, then if you still want to go you can get a job away from here."

"They can't keep me?" Jim fixed his eyes on Murdo's face. "You're sure they can't keep me?"

"I'm sure. Now don't you worry, Jim, boy, they won't touch you. It's going to be all right. We'll get you a coat and we'll go along together and don't you be scared—I'm going to be with you."

Wrapped in a coat too big for him Jim followed Murdo out into the dark. As long as Murdo was with him he knew he didn't need to worry. Murdo could tackle both Donald and Finlay. But Murdo would go home, Murdo would leave him, and what would happen then? That was what frightened Jim.

8. A New Deal

Alasdair Bàn and his band had landed up at Big Kenneth's house in the shelter of the hill, having searched the whole of Grasco to the Brae boundary. They were standing debating what to do next when they saw a man coming running up the road.

"It's Peter Stewart," said Archie Ross. "He'll have news, perhaps."

Peter arrived, panting. "We've got him—he was in Mackenzie's loft all the time."

"Well! the young rascal," exclaimed Alasdair. "And us searching in every burn and under every rock." The rest murmured agreement but were glad to be able to go home with a quiet mind.

"Come up to the house!" Peter urged Alasdair. "My father would never forgive me if I let you go home like that."

Old Kenneth, over eighty years of age, sat stooped in his chair, his white beard falling on his chest. He was delighted to hear first-hand news of the day's happenings. "A pity he didn't get clean away!" the old man growled. "If I had to live with the Bruces I'd go clean out of my mind, aye, and so would you, Alasdair, or any of us. I'm surprised the boy had so much spirit in him. I thought they had whipped it out of him years ago—he has the look of a half-starved dog. If he'd come here I'd have seen he got clean away."

"We couldn't keep him, Granpa, under their very noses!" protested his pretty granddaughter, Ishbel.

The old man winked at her. "There's ways and ways, my dear, with the sea at our door. We'd get him away to the navy and he'd come back an admiral. So, if he makes another bid for freedom we'll hide him here, eh, sweetheart?"

Ishbel giggled, Alasdair swallowed a large gulp of brandy which old Kenneth had ordered him to take to ward off the cold, and his daughter-in-law, Marion, said they would do nothing of the sort, they wouldn't be party to breaking the law. The boy must stay at home and do what his parents wished.

The old man began chuckling and wheezing and coughing. "We'll hide him under your bed, Marion, and even Donald wouldn't dare look for him there!"

Everyone laughed except Marion who blushed, saying, "Really, Granpa!" in a shocked tone.

"School!" went on the old man, in a voice of scorn. "What did you and me ever learn in school that was of use to us, Alasdair? The dates of the kings of England? Did that help you to make a good bargain? Aye, reckoning, of course, we had to learn *that* but what else? I left the school when I was just ten and made my way and knew my cattle—it would be a lot better for the boy to be up with you than wasting his time in that school."

"Aye! he has the makings of a good cattle man, he's keen for one thing and his eye is no' bad, that's another thing. All he needs is experience."

"And wasn't that what he was getting up in Brae? You've some nice cattle, I'm hearing." That, of course, set Alasdair off. Kenneth capped his yarns with his own, buying cattle here and there, knowing where to go for a bargain, knowing the dealer you could trust. It was late before Alasdair took his leave and made his way homeward by moonlight. The storm was over. He sorted out the day's events in his mind. Well, that would put paid to Jim's visits for a while, and he'd have to keep clear of the Bruces, that was clear, till they calmed down, anyway.

Well, he could get his messages at the forester's house. If he saw Jim he'd give him a piece of his mind for causing all that trouble and not telling him he was still at school.

Oddly enough the Bruces, for their part, made no special effort to keep the boy at home when he had finished his chores. They had been shaken by his sudden flight, more shaken than they liked to admit even to themselves. Murdo's words, "If you treat him rough he'll run off on you for good," had fallen on open ears. Donald saw that Sarah put more food on Jim's plate and Finlay told him tales of his youth as a docker on the Clyde and the terrible characters a man met once he left home. Strangely enough, too, the Bruces did not blame Alasdair for the whole affair as they might well have done. No, as they were incapable of blaming themselves, they picked on Murdo. It was a likely story that he hadn't known the boy was in his own byre! He had a brass neck to be swearing to them on the road out there that he knew nothing at all about Jim. And to cap all he had the face to come along and tell *them* how they should bring the boy up! That what he said was true did not make it sweeter for the Bruces. Worse still, there was something about Murdo, peaceable as he was by nature, which made them chary of starting a quarrel so their ill nature, finding no outlet, festered inside them.

Miss Menzies, at least, had won her battle. Jim came every day to school. He sat silent and apathetic in class but gave no trouble. She, on her side, left him alone as much as possible having no wish to drive him to further escapades.

Jim was troubled by a dream. It was always the same so that he knew when it began just what he had to go through. He was in a room crowded with people all talking at once. He guessed they were talking to keep him from noticing something but he knew that there was only one thing that mattered. The door! He must reach it before it was too late. But his feet dragged, they were so heavy he could hardly lift them, and while he struggled, he knew that his chances were slipping away, he would be too late. Too late for what? He didn't know, he didn't know, that was the worst of it! In the nightmare he reached the door at last, stretched upwards to grasp the knob, but he had taken too long, they were on to him, they were grabbing his fingers, forcing them to lose hold and all the time he was crying, "Don't leave me! Don't leave me!"

His own cries wakened him, he would lie trembling, bathed in sweat. Once or twice Finlay woke him, shaking him by the shoulder, saying, "What are you carrying on about? Can you not be quiet and let a man have peace in his bed?" When this happened Jim was so glad to be wakened that he did not mind Finlay's peevish complaints. "Is it raining, Finlay?" he would ask, or, "Has the wind changed? Has it gone round to the north?" or anything at all which would keep Finlay awake for a little till he could shake off the feeling of doom which lay upon his spirit.

In the daytime he slouched to school. That first day he had whispered to Tom, "Did your Dad beat you?" and was properly scornful when Tom said, "No!" He boasted of the weals on his back which he had managed to see with the aid of Sarah's hand mirror and the old, cracked looking-glass in his own bedroom.

"They're all over my back!" he boasted, taking off his jersey in the cart shed so that Tom could see with his own eyes. What he hid from Tom was that he had wept and cried but he couldn't hide it from himself. His pride hurt more than his sore back. He had meant to be so tough! He had been so pleased with himself, too, outwitting the Bruces and the school but both school and Bruces had caught up on him in the end. He had begun to feel that autumn as if a new life were in front of him. He had seen himself learning to know more about cattle, becoming alert to any sign of sickness, training his eye to know just when they would need hand feeding; all experience for some distant time when he, too, would have a place of his own, animals of his own. He had been within a jump of freedom but now the door had banged shut in his face. He was right back on the Bruces' croft. Worse still, he had lost his courage. He did what he was told, fetched drinking water from the spring, washing water from the stream, cleaned the byre, humped loads on his back, dragged hay from the tightly piled stacks and when there was absolutely nothing else to do he was made to pick stones off the top field to make it ready for spring ploughing. Up there he could have had a grand view of the whole township, of the loch and Brae closing it in to the south of Ben Mor, with one arm outspread to encircle the Corry Mor, but he would not look. He worked with his face to the Udale hill, gathering handfuls of stones and building them into small cairns at the edge of the field.

At school the children thought of him as a desperate character, capable of any wild act. A boy who could get out of a window on a stormy winter's night and sleep in a barn was clearly worthy of respect. They showed it by asking him to pick sides for football. When he refused and would not even play they were not deterred but asked him again next day. They lent him pencils and rubbers when, as usually happened, he had lost his own. But Jim, sunk in his own private misery, hardly noticed. Even Tom could not get him to join in ferreting, which they had often done together on winter Saturdays. One Friday evening Tom took Jim to see the ferrets in their box, told him the nets were ready, and asked him to come along in the morning. They would try the hill above the crofts where rabbits were very plentiful. But Jim only shook his head, he couldn't be bothered. Since he was forbidden to go to Brae, since Alasdair didn't care about him, he would just stay at home.

The school closed with the usual Christmas party. In all his time at school Sarah had never allowed him to go to the party because he had no party clothes.

A New Deal

He had always longed to join in the fun but now he didn't care. Parties were for kids. He, Jim, was all but grown-up.

Then something happened to stir him out of his unnatural apathy.

They were at supper one evening when Donald remarked that he had met Alasdair Bàn on the road and he had said he was going home for New Year. This was a blow to Jim. He had been hoping, without even admitting it to himself, that he would meet Alasdair during the holidays and then Alasdair would invite him up as he used to do. Worse news was to follow.

"I hear Alec John's looking after the cattle for him," Donald went on. "Why couldn't you get the job for yourself? You were so friendly with Alasdair."

"That's what he thought!" Sarah gibed. "But he didn't think so much of you when he asked Alec John and not you!"

To have them goading him for not doing what he longed to do was almost too much to bear. "But—but——" he stammered. "*You* didn't want me to go to Brae——"

"There's no school the now," replied Donald, "and you could have earned some money for your keep, but seemingly he'd sooner have Alec John."

It wasn't true! Jim knew it wasn't true. Alec John didn't know the cattle as Jim did! He wouldn't know one from the other, he'd never notice if one fell sick. Oh! this was too much, this was more than he could bear.

Next morning, having done all his chores, and with a hunk of bread in his pocket, he took the Brae path. There were no cattle to be seen. Obviously Alasdair would have left them near Brae as he wouldn't expect Alec John to be an early riser. Reaching the place where the path divided Jim went up towards the Corry Mor thinking in this way he would have a better idea where all the beasts were. Sure enough, before he had gone very far he came on a dozen, some just getting to their feet, stretching their legs. There had been frost in the night which had rimed their coats, their breath formed little clouds on the still, cold air. Jim recognised old friends but was careful not to disturb them. They were fine where they were. He crossed the Corry Mor meeting groups here and there and by the time he had reached Brae he had seen them all. The sun was shining brightly everywhere except on the cottage which lay in shadow.

Jim tried the door and found it was not locked so he walked in. Everything was neat as a pin in the kitchen, dishes all on the shelves, a bundle of kindling lying by the hearth ready to make a fire, the herring basket full of peats. In the bedroom the bed had been made, a candle stood in the candlestick beside the bed. There was a faint smell of Alasdair's tobacco still in the air. The smell brought Alasdair vividly to Jim's mind. He thought of all the fun they had had and of all the good meals Alasdair had cooked. Sarah, he now knew, could not cook. When she made a stew the meat floated in water, her soups were wishy-washy with nothing but lumps of turnip in the stock. He stared at the empty grate. No more meals! Alasdair had given him up. He'd taste no more rabbit stews with onion nor lick his fingers after a pot roast of mutton.

Just then he heard a dog bark. He went out at once to see Alec John driving the whole herd up towards Brae. The silly sausage! There hadn't been the slightest need to disturb the beasts which had been just grand where they were. Now he had put every one of them off grazing, of all the stupid idiots! The dog was barking madly. It was that brute, Paddy, who had even less sense than his master. Jim set off at a run. He wasn't going to let Alasdair's cattle be driven like that. He reached the bank of the Corry Mor burn just as the whole herd came charging down on the far side, helter-skelter, the ones behind using their horns freely on the ones in front.

"Stop!" Jim shouted furiously. "Stop!" But Alec John paid no attention. He was enjoying himself fine, likening himself to one of those cowboys who were always galloping after cattle on horseback. He hadn't got a horse but he was going as fast as he could. He went on urging Paddy, a big, raw-boned, russet-coloured tyke, to harass the herd and Paddy was delighted to do so. He jumped up on them, nipping their tails and even swinging on them. Jim, after months of Alasdair's training, was shocked to the core. He ran across the footbridge and grabbed Alec John by the arm. "What are you up to? Are you daft?"

This annoyed Alec John. "I'm not daft! I'm putting up the cattle the way Alasdair Bàn told me and I'll thank you, Jim Smith, to clear off and let me get on with the business."

"I'll do no such thing!" Jim retorted. "I'm not standing by and seeing you breaking their legs. There! Look at that! What did I tell you?"

He pointed to a bonny cross-highland heifer which had charged into a bog and was floundering desperately.

Alec John was not a bit dismayed. "I'll get her out with Paddy!" he cried.

This was too much for Jim. "Get out of here!" he yelled. "You and your Paddy, and if I see you here again I'll beat the living daylight out of you."

Alec John, though scared by now, was not going to give in without a struggle.

"You mind your own business!" he shouted above the bellowing of the herd. "I'm in charge here and not you. Alasdair Bàn asked me and not you—so there!"

He put his fingers to his lips and whistled, the last sound he made before landing in the bog with Jim on top of him. He did his best even then but it was a bad place for a fight. Even as he writhed and kicked he felt himself sinking in the black slime. Jim forced his head back till the mud crept into his ears. The feeling was so horrid that Alec John cried, panic stricken, "Let me up! Let me up!"

"Will you go home?"

"Yes! Yes!"

"And you won't tell a soul? Not your father, not your mother, not Ewen——"

"Oh! stop it, Jim, I told you—nobody."

"Word of honour?"

"Yes! Cut my throat if I tell a soul. Let me go!"

Jim got off him, dragged him clear of the bog, and helped him to wash off some, at least, of the mud in the burn. They were both quite matter of fact. Jim was thinking hard, then he said, "Look, Alec John, I don't want the money—you can keep it so you'll have to look as if you were doing the work. Come a bit along the lochside in the mornings and evenings. That'll make them think it's all right but don't you put a finger on the cattle. Do you understand that?" Alec John nodded sulkily. During the fight the heifer had managed to get clear of the bog on her own and was standing panting, her beautiful curly coat all stained with mud and green slime. The sight of her roused Jim's ire once more.

"Some herdsman you are!" he jeered. "You and your Paddy." The latter was sitting, his long red tongue hanging out, oozing self-satisfaction. Jim looked at him with distaste. How unlike Glen he was. "Oh! get off! the pair of you—and mind what I say for if I see you interfering with the beasts or moving them one inch, either you or that lumbering jackass over there, I'll put you back in the bog and I'll sit on you till you go under and there's nothing left but a few bubbles!"

In spite of himself Alec John shuddered for he was convinced that Jim would do exactly what he threatened. He took to his heels but when he had put a fair distance between himself and his enemy he shouted, "Oh! you are a silly ass doing all that for nothing! Silly ass!" He broke off short when he saw Jim was coming after him, ran and ran till he was out of breath, but when he looked back Jim was driving the cattle gently up towards the Corry Mor.

So Jim remained in possession of the field. Early in the morning he made sure that none was near the forestry drains and last thing in the evening he drove them quietly along the side of the loch to a safe place for the night.

"What are you going up to Brae for when Alec John's in charge?" Donald asked him irritably. "Can you not leave Brae alone?"

"Oh! I'm just taking a look," Jim replied, a bit embarrassed. "Alec John doesn't know much about cattle."

"Oh! doesn't he? And you think you know a lot, eh?"

Jim prudently sang dumb. "I don't go till all the work's done," he muttered.

" Huh! " was all Donald said. He didn't want more trouble and it was true the boy did what little work there was in the short winter days. If he liked to waste his time wandering up to Brae what did it matter? Sarah thought otherwise.

" You'll see how it'll turn out," she would say, pleating folds in her wide black skirt. " Let him go now and you won't be able to stop him again. When that happens don't say I didn't tell you."

" Leave the boy alone! " her husband answered angrily. " If you had it your way he'd be gone already. I know what I'm doing and just you leave him alone."

So Sarah sat stroking the black cat till it purred with delight, arching its back. " You'll see, you'll see! " she murmured, but Donald would not heed her.

Jim had been passing the time up at Brae by setting Alasdair's rabbit snares. On the very last morning he succeeded in catching one and went down the hill to the cottage proudly swinging the dead beast by the back legs. He gutted it, tied the back legs, and hung it at the back of the door. That'll surprise him, he thought. He'll wonder where that came from! He sat down in Alasdair's chair and gazed at the rabbit and then at the fire. What if he skinned it, cooked it, and left it at the side of the fire ready for Alasdair's supper? He'd be home by six or seven o'clock at the latest. A hot supper would be a nice welcome home. He still hesitated a little because he had never cooked anything in his life but finally he jumped to his feet. He'd go ahead and if the dish wasn't tasty why, the dogs could have it. For the next half hour he was very busy indeed for first of all the fire gave him trouble, the peats producing more smoke than flame till at last, with the aid of sticks, he got them to burn properly. He cut his finger skinning the rabbit and blood dripped over everything. He hadn't a hanky but found an old rag, twisted it round his finger, and tied it with one hand and his teeth. After that he cut the rabbit into small pieces and then remembered that

Alasdair rolled them in flour. He searched in all the tins in vain, he'd just have to stew them as they were. A pity, that! He was dropping the pieces into the stew pan when Alasdair walked in. Jim stood staring at him, his jaw dropping and the blood rushing into his cheeks.

"Well, Jim, here's a surprise, indeed! Who would have expected to see you here?" exclaimed Alasdair cheerfully, as he shot a quick look at his disordered kitchen which he had left so spick and span in true sailor fashion. His remark increased poor Jim's confusion for, as he well knew, he had no right to be there and worse still, he had chased home the rightful herdboy and now he had been caught making free with Alasdair's stores, his peats, his pots, and pans. He couldn't find a word to say. The two dogs had come in each after his own fashion, Glen going straight to his own corner and Spot having a quick "recce" to see what he could find.

"Away and lie down!" he was told. He slunk under a chair. Alasdair went on talking about the fine spell of weather for the time of year, how good the cattle were looking, the ones he had seen on his way up at any rate. Jim stood silent, his hands hanging by his side, his head half averted. He didn't hear a word the man was saying for the confusion of his own mind.

"What are you making?" Alasdair asked. This time Jim managed to say "rabbit" in a sort of croak.

"Did you catch it yourself? Well, that's a treat. I could do with a right feed. Was it a good one?" Jim only nodded.

"We'll put the other bits in," said Alasdair, taking charge. "You find the lid, boy, and did you salt it?" No, he hadn't. Alasdair remedied that and put the pot to simmer. He then took off his raincoat, searched for his pipe, and settled himself comfortably by the fire. Jim saw that his way to the door was clear. "I'll be going," he mumbled.

"Heh! what for?"

But Jim was only intent on getting away. He was through the first door but was hindered by the second and Alasdair had time to catch him and draw him back into the kitchen.

"Why, Jim," he protested, "that's not friendly, lad. Sit down, sit down and tell me what's wrong."

Alasdair's voice was so friendly and kind that Jim found it harder than ever to voice his complaints. Seeing this Alasdair grasped the nettle. "Is it because I asked Alec John and not you to look after the cattle? Is that what's bothering you?" Jim nodded. "But, look, Jim, what else could I do?" he went on in his most persuasive voice, that voice which was his greatest asset and had taken pounds off the price of any beast he wanted to buy and put pounds on to the price of every beast he sold. "Weren't they threatening me with going to court over you? I didn't dare go near them although it was you I wanted all the time for you know the cattle and I can trust you, but I was sure your father wouldn't let you come so what could I do?"

"They didn't mind," Jim interrupted him. "They said I could have earned some money and when you took Alec John instead of me they laughed at me saying you thought I was no use——" His voice quavered, and he stopped abruptly.

"Well, for any favour, if that doesn't beat the band!" exclaimed Alasdair. "The last time I saw Donald and Finlay they were telling me I had ruined you and how was I to know that the wind had shifted? But if I *had* known I'd never have passed your door."

A core of resentment still lay in Jim's heart. "You could have tried!"

"So I could!" replied Alasdair, relighting his pipe which had gone out during these explanations. "But if I *had* there's no saying but they would have refused. To tell the truth, lad, I don't like taking 'no' for an answer and that's what sent me to the Macdonalds. How did Alec John get on?"

Jim gave a derisive snort. "He was no use! If you'd seen

him! Why, he almost made the cows in calf drop them that very first day."

"You don't say!" said Alasdair, sucking hard on the stem of his pipe. Then the whole story of Alec John and the infamous Paddy came bursting out. "But I saved them!" Jim concluded. "And I told him to clear off home."

"Well, well!" was all Alasdair could find to say as he drew on his pipe for comfort.

Jim, stealing a look at him, for once read his thoughts. "It's all right," he said a little stiffly, "you don't need to worry about the Macdonalds. I told him not to tell and that he'd get paid just the same. Well, I'd better go now." He got to his feet.

"Och! don't go, Jim, don't hold it against me, boy." Alasdair was almost pleading now. "Do you know this? I wasn't easy in my mind, I kept thinking, perhaps that boy will do the beasts a harm. I told my mother if it was you I'd left in charge I could have slept last night at home but as it was I came away and reached Satran last night—I stayed with the Martins—you remember Mary?—and then took the road first thing in the morning because I was afraid there might be something wrong." Alasdair invented this tale as he went along. In fact, he had left home the night before because he had been offered a lift but he began to believe his tale himself, especially when he saw Jim's face light up and heard him say, "And if it had been me you wouldn't have come?"

"That's right, sure as I'm here."

Jim's smile broke through. "Well! they're all right, they're fine, I've seen the whole lot every day."

"Well, Jim, that's grand, you've been a great help. Why, I was saying to Mary only last night what a grand hand you were getting to be, for she was asking after you." Jim was pleased to be remembered. He, himself, would always remember Mary. She had looked so round and comfortable and her little house was so cosy. Alasdair was busy chewing over some problem. "I'll need to pay you, boy," he said, but Jim explained that Sarah took anything he ever made. "Aye! well, I'll give her something and I'll keep something for you here. It'll be like having it in the bank and when you want it you've only to ask." That was fine but the money had been the least of Jim's worries.

Before they separated that evening it was agreed between them that he was to come up whenever he was free but he was not to play truant any more and he was to do all his foster-parents asked of him. "You'll promise me that, Jim, won't you?" The firelight played on the boy's face lighting up his earnest expression.

"I promise," he said. They solemnly shook hands on the bargain and Jim ran home happier than he had been for many a day.

9. Cows and Calves

That's how it was, then, through the winter and into the spring. School every day, work on the croft, and only when everything had been done did Jim take the road to Brae. Sometimes this meant he had both Saturdays and Sundays free but more often it meant Sundays only. But Jim did not rebel. So long as he was sure of Sunday he had something to look forward to all week and something to look back on, too, when there were too many days between him and the following Sunday.

Alasdair made full use of him when he did go up. In the last weeks of winter the wind blew steadily from the east. It was cold, it was dry, and the island took on its bleakest look, wearied and washed out by winter. More and more of the herd required hand feeding. Every Sunday Alasdair and Jim climbed the steep slope behind the cottage, carrying a sack of oilcake and a bundle of tin basins.

" Never make a habit of feeding your animals in the same place," Alasdair told him. " It's easier for yourself, of course, but it's not good for them. They'll come looking for it and stand around waiting instead of doing the best they can for themselves. I go looking for them every day and feed them where I find them."

Sometimes they were beside the shore at the ruins of an old fort or down in the one bay on that part of the coast where they rooted among the seaweed, chewing bones and other rubbish tossed up by the tide. Again they might have to go to the foot of the cliffs which rose almost vertically 300 feet above the surf. As soon as they appeared the herd came running.

"Quick! Down with the basins, Jim." Jim spread them out in a long line and Alasdair filled each with the day's ration of linseed cake. Cattle have no table manners so it is the herdsman's job to see that each gets its fair share and that the smaller and weaker are not pushed aside by their stronger companions. To begin with Jim used too much strength and a beast driven out of the wrong dish would charge along the line creating havoc. "Oh! go easy, man!" Alasdair would protest at such clumsy conduct. "Give them a smack with your hand, not a blow with your stick. You're only making bad worse." But it took Jim a little time to learn the knack. Formerly, Alasdair had lavished praise on the boy for even recognising a beast, now he abused him roundly if he made any mistake. This upset Jim a little till he came to understand that Alasdair was raising the standard only because his pupil was learning fast.

The cows were due to calve any day, the little white one first, Alasdair said, and then the yellow one with the white star on her forehead. "But I don't know," he would say with a shake of the head, watching the oilcake disappear, "that they're worth their keep. Look at the oilcake they're eating and they'll be needing it right up to May to keep them in milk so that they do the calves well. I believe I'd be better to keep two-year-old bullocks. Look at these fellows over there getting on grand without a bite from us." It always amused Jim to see the bullocks lift their heads when the others went cantering off to receive their rations. They would gaze in a kind of mild surprise as if to say, "What's all this carry-on?" But in a few moments they would drop their heads again and get back to the business of keeping themselves alive.

There was one Sunday Jim always remembered. Indeed, he hadn't much chance to forget it with Alasdair around. They had climbed up and had come upon the cattle farther off than usual. They went through the routine and it was only when he had every beast eating its own portion that Jim noticed there was one basin too many. He looked again at every beast and then shouted to Alasdair, " The wee white cow's missing ! " Alasdair nodded. When the oilcake had been eaten he and Jim walked on till they came to the next burn running in a slight hollow down to the sea.

" There she is ! " cried Jim. Of all the cattle he liked the wee cow best because he had met her that day up in the mist when he hardly knew Alasdair and had no idea of what Brae would come to mean to him.

Alasdair called, " *Shu bheag, shu bheag* ! " but instead of coming the little cow only mooed softly back and flapped her large ears. Alasdair filled a basin and gave it to Jim who went towards her casually and set the basin down. He was just straightening up when he heard a rush of hoofs and the next second he found himself rolling down the bank with the little cow snorting belligerently right above him. He was so surprised he gaped at her, noting the funny black smudges round her mouth when the sight of her preparing to charge sent him with one bound across the burn and scrambling up the bank. He could hear Alasdair giving vent to an enormous laugh and this didn't please him one bit. Why, he'd almost been gored and all Alasdair could do was laugh ! " Oh ! boy, you'll need to move quicker than that ! " he was saying between chuckles. " Has she calved, Jim ? "

" No ! " he said and stepped into a clump of bracken. Something broke out from under his feet. Quite unnerved by these happenings Jim uttered a yell and leapt into the air. " Oh ! *gu siorruidh*, what was that ? " he exclaimed, looking to Alasdair for guidance, but the latter was rolling on the grass quite helpless with mirth and ten yards away a very small yellow calf was bellowing its dismay.

" Oh ! oh ! Losh ! " was all Jim could find to say.

Alasdair hiccuped, " Oh, no, she hasn't calved, oh! no," and went off into another peal of laughter.

Jim blushed and fidgeted. He had thought it was the devil himself jumping up from under his feet. " Do you mean to say you knew she had calved? " he asked.

Alasdair wiped his streaming eyes. " Oh! man, you've got a lot to learn. Knew? Why, of course I knew she had either calved already or was calving when she wouldn't come to me. These highland cows, they're wild in their ways. They hide their calves just the way deer do and the calf won't move till she comes to it. Look where she had it, in a nest of bracken, as cosy as you please. Oh! Jim, lad, your face! It was as good as a play. That's the best laugh I've had in many a day."

Jim looked at the little object recovering its composure by sucking its mother and smiled, if reluctantly. He might as well enjoy the joke against himself for it was evidently going to last Alasdair a very long time.

One Saturday Jim found Alasdair in the forester's house. He was too shy to go in but waited patiently at the door with Glen and Spot till Mrs. Grant, happening to go out for coal, saw him and insisted that he should go inside. He slipped into a seat at the back of the room and hoped that Alasdair wouldn't stay chatting long with all those people.

" It was a grand hill for wedders," Alasdair was saying, " and it's a great pity to see it going under trees." The workers were busy that spring planting the tiny trees in the ground made ready for them.

" Aye, a pity, right enough," Murdo Mackenzie agreed. " We can't eat trees."

Charlie Grant snorted. " You and your sheep! What's a sheep fetching to-day? And your wool? Tenpence a pound, is it? You should be thanking Providence the Forestry came when it did and started paying you wages or you wouldn't know by now how to pay the rent! The ground here is sheep sick. Look at your crofts!" He brandished an arm across the river. "Not a blade of grass over there! And on this side, free of the sheep, the grass is pushing up everywhere."

"It seems a waste with nothing eating it," commented Ewen Macdonald.

"Well, there's Alasdair's cattle, they'll eat the rough stuff which the sheep you're so fond of won't and that's what does the damage in the long run."

"In the old days they turned men off for sheep and now they are turning sheep off for trees," said Ewen thoughtfully.

"That's so, sheep for *trees*, but we're not turning men off— we're taking them *on*. You had one shepherd in the old days for Brae and another for this hirsel, Grasco—two men!— Instead of two men you'll have a dozen working here before long, a squad of men, planting, brashing, thinning, and finally cutting."

"For a wee while, maybe," assented Alasdair. "But then there'll be nothing to do but watch them grow—you'll be a while reaching the cutting stage."

"Aye, and it'll be a while before we reach the Brae boundary! Look at the money it's bringing into the place, man! 'You can't eat trees.' Who's asking you to but you can turn your wages into food, eh?"

Jim wriggled on his hard seat. He was bored with all this talk. Of course, Alasdair and the rest were right and Grant was wrong. Mrs. Grant made him a sandwich and this brought Grant's attention on to him.

"And look at Jim there! He'll be wanting work when he leaves school, won't you, Jim?" Jim blushed because they were all looking at him.

"I don't want to work at the forestry," he said.

"Good on you, lad!" exclaimed Alasdair, delighted to have Grant cut off in mid-flow, but Charlie wasn't easily beaten. Having lost Jim he turned on Ewen.

" What's all this I hear about you getting married, Ewen? "

Ewen blushed crimson and made them all laugh. " Well, I might be," he replied cautiously, rather as if it was not directly his concern.

" And you'll settle in Udale? "

" Aye, I might."

" But if the Forestry hadn't come you couldn't have settled here, isn't that so? "

" I was thinking of going to sea but I'd rather have sheep than trees for all that."

Charlie laughed and groaned. " There's no pleasing you but I'll come and dance at your wedding all the same."

At last Alasdair got under way and Jim went gleefully with him. He had a problem on his mind and wanted Alasdair's advice.

" It's the cows," he explained. " *Their* cows, Bluebell and Snowdrop. It was the other night I noticed them properly. They're as thin as rakes, but the funny thing is they don't even eat the food we give them and you'd think if they were as hungry as all that they'd eat anything."

Alasdair shook his head. " That old hay! It was under the rain for weeks. You might as well feed them on sawdust. Do they give them trusk? Or oilcake? Or meal drinks? Or put treacle on the hay? They need something to sweeten it."

Jim shook his head to all this. " They don't give them anything but hay."

" Well, they'll lose them, then, you can take my word for that. It's this dry spell after a bad autumn and a bad harvest. I tell you what, Jim, I'll come down on Monday and take a look myself. I'll say I want to see the stirks and that way I have an excuse for looking at the cows."

Jim was astonished that he minded about the cows. He had always hated both Bluebell and Snowdrop for the trouble they gave him but since Alasdair had taught him to look after cattle he found he didn't like to see any beast not thriving for lack of care.

"The thing is," he said doubtfully, "they're so mean they won't want to spend any money on them."

"Maybe they'll listen to me," said Alasdair. "I'll come down anyway." He was as good as his word. The cows had come early to the byre door. It was quite true what Jim had said, the animals were just a ruckle of bones and hadn't the heart left to find food for themselves on the hill. Alasdair came straight to the point. "You'll lose these cows unless you give them trusk or oilcake."

At once the brothers began protesting that the cows were leaving the hay in their stalls and, therefore, they were getting enough. Alasdair dealt quickly with that one. "That hay!" he said scornfully. "In a good year it would hardly do as bedding."

Sarah had come out to listen and here she began to wail,

109

whether because the cows might die or because they were being asked to spend money it was hard to say.

"These are good, soft cows, that were on good places," Alasdair went on, unperturbed. "They're not like some of these hardy brutes that can live on a bite of heather. Your cows are well bred and good milkers so you have to be good to them."

"Oh! they're beautiful cows," Sarah agreed. "Beautiful, the very best. You should see the cream—you could float half a crown on it——"

"Well, then," retorted Alasdair firmly but kindly, "order bags of trusk for them from the distillery and till you get them keep giving them meal drinks and get some treacle and put it on the hay. That way they'll try and eat it, poor brutes."

"Och! I'm sure it's the best of hay!" cried Finlay, cut to the heart at the thought of spending money.

"The hay is useless," said Alasdair calmly, "just packing, that's all. But have it your own way. Another week of starvation and you can be digging a hole in the ground for them, Finlay."

This brought forth a volley of, "Obh! Obh! Obh!" from Sarah. She took Alasdair into the house and made tea for him and promised to follow his instructions to the letter. She was all over him. Was his tea sweet enough? Would he have another slice of loaf bread? She'd always heard that there was no one in the island with an eye for cattle like himself! Oh! she'd heard that ages ago and now she knew it was true.

Jim sat in the background and marvelled. Here she was as sweet as syrup yet, within an hour of Alasdair's departure, she'd be miscalling him for all she was worth, he'd take a bet on it. Which was what she did, while she milked the cow with one hand and held the quart jug in the other, an old-fashioned way of milking. She should have milked with both hands, putting the pail down on the ground. Jim was waiting to feed the calves and by that time Sarah hadn't left a feather on Alasdair's back.

He was nothing but a glib tongue, he was a lazy fellow just taking advantage of Jim, just making use of him. Jim was too stupid to know his own friends. But all this running up to Brae would have to stop. There was the dung to spread and the fields to plough and harrow, potatoes to plant. Jim would have to stay at home.

The boy listened in silence. Yes, he knew he'd not get away on Saturdays for a time but there was always Sunday. So long as they couldn't take that from him he was content.

10. Going for the Doctor

The Easter holidays had come and gone. Work on the crofts was over for the time being, lambers were out on the hills, and the rest of the township went peat-cutting. On this particular morning every able-bodied person was off early, carrying provisions for the day and a kettle to brew tea. But Jim had first to take Snowdrop, the big black cow, now fully recovered, to the bull park which lay above the Lodge. Having seen the cow safely into the park and the gate secured he came back by the Lodge. He had seen the children pass by in the cart already so the silence all around did not surprise him. But then he heard an odd noise from the house. What had it been? A groan? Or his imagination playing him tricks? No, he heard it again. He pushed open the back door and there in the kitchen he could see Mrs. Mackenzie bent double, her head on the table. She didn't know he was there and groaned again. "Are you ill?" Jim asked awkwardly. She raised her head.

"Oh! it's you, Jim. I thought—everybody—gone——" she whispered. "I'm right bad." Another spasm took her, sweat stood out on her forehead, and the knuckles of the hand clasping the table edge grew white. The boy felt his ignorance deeply. What should he do? What would a grown-up do? There wasn't a soul left in the township except old Flora Stewart who was deaf and crippled with rheumatism. "Get the doctor, Jim," he heard Mrs. Mackenzie whisper. "I'm right bad. Get the doctor!" That was something he could do, indeed! The doctor's house lay some four miles away by road but if he took the short-cut over the hill the distance was cut by a mile.

"I'll go," he said. "I'm going, you hold on. I'll bring him quick."

He hurried out and was passing the cart shed when he saw a cycle. What about taking it? Would he be quicker riding the bicycle round the road or cutting across the moor on his feet? Even while he tried to calculate, his hands had seized the handle-bars and his feet were searching for the pedals. It was an old boneshaker belonging to Murdo. When he sat on the saddle his feet could not reach the pedals so he stood on them instead and went fast to the far end of the township. He was just making up his mind to keep on cycling when a hiss of escaping air told him the back tyre was punctured. There was nothing for it but to leave the bike at the roadside and to strike off across the moor.

Although he had never gone that way he knew the doctor's house lay near the head of the next loch and he thought he could judge pretty well the shortest way to it. Now his many journeys to Brae in all weathers stood him in good stead. He could do that journey—two and a half miles of rough going—in a little over forty minutes. He set himself to beat that pace now for some-one's life was in the balance, but he knew enough to start off at a fairly easy pace. What was needed was steady going to the top of the hill and after that he could afford to run. He was already above Stewart's croft where it nestled in the lap of the hill. He climbed with head bent, zigzagging as shepherds do up the steep slope. Once on the top, moor lay ahead, with bogs here and there. These he skirted where he could, plunging through them, however, when to go round would put him off his course, jumping from tussock to tussock of coarse grass. Once he misjudged his distance and fell back into the stagnant, peaty water. It was dirty but it cooled him. He jogged on hope-fully, fully expecting to come to the end of the moor and the descent on the far side at any moment, but still it stretched ahead

and after a while doubts began to gnaw him. Was he taking the quickest way? Perhaps if he had followed the road he would have got a lift and have been already at the doctor's, but it was too late to think of that now. Sweat ran into his eyes and blinded him. He pulled off his jersey and the sun beat down on his bare arms and shoulders.

He stopped to take his bearings. His breath was rasping in his throat, he could hear the blood pounding in his ears, and his hair was plastered to his head with sweat. The great mass of the Coolins lay to the south-east, every rock shining in the sun. From there his eye travelled northwards and he saw a deep ravine lying ahead of him. He realised he had come too far, for there was no ravine between him and the doctor's, so he slewed to the left, knowing he had wasted precious minutes. Oh! if he had only crossed the hill before. The difference between life

and death might hang on his speed. He ran on but now he had a stitch in his side.

Tom's mother, he thought. Funny, I can't remember my own mother. I used to think she'd come for me, she'd come in a car and I'd be waiting. She'd pick me up, quick, and run with me to the car, we'd escape together, and no one would separate us any more. Of course, he had given up that nonsense long ago. No one had ever come, no one ever would. All at once he saw the sea loch lying below him, the sun sparkling on the water. He broke into a run. There! There! Right below him he saw the doctor's house with its line of fir trees to break the wind. He hadn't done so badly after all. He pounded down the last slope and just then he picked up the sound of a car's engine being revved. Suppose the doctor was going out! Suppose he couldn't catch him! This new fear drove him on, forcing his labouring legs to go still faster. He scrambled wildly through the old wire fence at the foot of the field and then fell flat, entangled in a loose strand of barbed wire. This last misfortune was almost too much for him but he got to his knees, shouting and waving his arms, as the doctor's car came out of the gateway. The barbed wire gashed his leg as he struggled to free himself but he hardly felt it for he heard the doctor shouting and knew that he had been seen. Even then he could hardly believe it and ran to the car, clutching the window and gasping, " Oh! come quick, please come quick."

" Which way?" was all the doctor said. Jim pointed up the road. " Get in, then, get in, you're played out." Jim blundered round the car and stumbled into the seat. He felt very strange, almost light-headed. " Sit quiet," the doctor ordered him, turning the car uphill. He had covered a mile before he asked where he was to go. " Udale? Humph, yes, I thought you must be from there when I saw you running down the hill. You the Bruces' boy?"

" I'm Jim Smith," the boy replied, for he felt the name set him apart from the Bruces.

" What time was it when you left the Lodge?"

" I don't know—it was early."

" It's early yet, boy, only half past ten." He said no more, concentrating on making the car go as fast as possible on the narrow, rutted road. Jim gripped the seat nervously as they roared down the hill and through the empty township, scattering the hens sunbathing in the dust and sending them squawking off in terror. In front of the Lodge the doctor jumped out. " Wait," he said, " I may need help." All at once everything was very quiet. No sound anywhere, only the sunlight streaming down on old grey walls, on the trees, motionless, their green translucent leaves shimmering against the blue sky. It wasn't a day for sickness. But what if Tom's mother had died when he was away? People *did* die quickly sometimes, he knew. He felt the minutes like hours and the car like a cage. He got out, but even as he did so the doctor appeared supporting Tom's mother with one arm. " Open the back door, boy," he ordered.

Mrs. Mackenzie smiled faintly at Jim, saying, " You *were* quick." They were off once more but this time the doctor drove carefully, avoiding potholes.

" Do you want off at your house? " he asked Jim.

" No, everyone's at the peats," he replied.

" Everyone? Well, find Murdo, then, and tell him I'm taking his wife to Broadford Hospital. It's acute appendicitis, and we'll have to operate at once."

" I'll tell him," Jim said and indeed, he felt very important as he trudged across the quarter mile of moor to reach the peat cutters. Murdo's bog lay nearest. Murdo saw him coming and stopped working, taking out his big red hanky to wipe his face.

" Well, Jim, lad, it's warm. Was that the doctor's car? It looked a bit like his."

" Yes, it's his. He's taking your wife to hospital," Jim said quickly.

Murdo stopped wiping his face and gazed at Jim. " My wife? My wife? Taking her to hospital? But she was all right when I left—she was going to follow us——" he broke off in perplexity.

" Daddy! Daddy! What is it? " Mary asked, running up to him. " Where's Mother? " But Murdo began putting on his jacket without replying. It was as if he wasn't really there. "What's wrong, Daddy? " Mary asked again, but more anxiously. Still he said nothing. If the words reached him their sense did not. He had his old blue jacket on by now and stood looking at his hands all streaked with wet peat. Feeling the tension all round her little Susan began to cry. She had never seen her father look like that, so blank and blind. Her crying roused him.

" I'll have to go," he said hastily, and added to Tom, who stood below him in the bog where he had been throwing out the wet

117

peat. "Look after the children, Tom, I must go to your mother." He turned his back on them without more ado and strode off across the moor. Nan's little face crumpled and tears poured silently down her cheeks. She did not know what was wrong but she felt her father's anxiety and grief.

Tom jumped out of the bog, found a dry spot, and took the small children on his knee, saying, "Don't cry, now, don't cry, I'll look after you."

"What *happened*, Jim? What's wrong with Mother?" asked Donnie. Jim told his story quickly. He could see the Bruces staring over at him and presently Donald came marching over and began berating him without waiting for an explanation.

"What are you meaning, boy, is this the time you come to work?"

"It's Tom's mother," Jim explained. "She was taken ill and I had to get the doctor."

"Did the doctor say Mother was very bad, Jim?" Tom asked.

"It's acute appendicitis, he had to take her to Broadford."

"Well! well! that's not so good," said Donald. "But come away, now, Finlay can't get on without you." Finlay was ready with his share of the scolding but his brother cut him short for once.

"Appendicitis!" cried Sarah, from where she stood in the bog. "It's more likely a touch of the colic!"

Jim was kept busy throwing out the long black peats Finlay cut with the *cas chrom*—the instrument used for this work only, but he noticed Kursty Morag, Hugh's wife, leave her work and cross over to Murdo's bog. She brought the children back with her and gave them tea. The little ones soon cheered up and built little houses with old, dry peat. In the evening Ewen and Tom between them managed to catch Sally and put her in the cart. Then all the children piled in and Ewen led the mare home. Jim longed to go with them. He was so tired he could scarcely throw a peat straight but Finlay went on cutting with a tireless, rhythmic stroke which Jim could hardly keep up with. When the brothers at last decided to stop Jim had been bent so long he could scarcely straighten himself and felt dizzy. Even when they reached home after plodding nearly two miles there were still the cows to fetch and calves to feed. Small wonder that he slept soundly that night and did not waken till late the following morning.

Sarah, while serving the men, told story after story of people who had died " under the knife," as she phrased it, particularly when having operations for appendicitis. Jim listened with a sinking heart. If the operation was as bad as that then Tom's mother would never come home! Murdo had not come back and things looked bad.

When he was free he stood for a little while hesitating by the roadside wondering whether he should go to the Lodge. But he was afraid of being there when, or if, bad news came. In the end he took the Brae path.

Ever since New Year he had made a point of being early in Brae on Sundays and of taking any cattle he found too near the forestry drains along with him. So, after many months of this Alasdair didn't worry his head about cattle on that day. But this morning Jim had slept in and when he rounded a corner what should he see but five of the big bullocks eating happily and treading under them the tiny trees. Jim began to run but at that very moment Alasdair came in sight. He waved his stick and at once the two dogs fell upon the animals and had them out of the trees and back on the road before Jim had even caught up. But then Alasdair swung round on him, saying angrily, " And a fine herdsman you are! Just look at the mess these brutes have made. I won't be able to show my face at the forester's, thanks to you! What in the world came over you?"

Jim began to stammer as he always did when he was excited

or upset. Alasdair went off after the cattle, not waiting for an explanation and Jim followed slowly in his rear. His whole body ached from the exertions of the day before. Added to that his arms and shoulders had been burnt by the sun and were very sore. The gashes on his leg made by the barbed wire throbbed and he had a blister on his heel. He trailed slowly along the path, not because he wanted to go to Brae but rather because he didn't know what else to do. His heel, however, became so painful that he sat down by the side of the path and peeled off his stocking. He was just opposite the Lodge and he sat looking across and wishing he could see Tom. He felt in a strange mood as if the events of the day before had jolted him out of a set way of behaving. For the last nine months he had thought of nothing but Brae and cattle. He had had no time for Tom, never so much as giving him a thought outside school hours. They hadn't gone ferreting together all winter, they hadn't taken their hazel rods and gone fishing small brown trout up the burn even once that summer. He spent every moment he had free with Alasdair. But sitting there in the hot sunshine, looking across the bright waters of the loch to the old, grey Lodge behind its screen of elms, he remembered all the kindnesses he had been shown there, how Murdo's wife had made him sit close to the big range on cold winter mornings, how she had dried his clothes, clothing him meanwhile in Tom's, he remembered the thick, white oven scones she had given him, just newly baked, making the butter melt inside them, he remembered the games he and Tom had played in the steading, the dens they had had from which they sallied forth, crawling across rafters, sliding down ropes, pouncing on unsuspecting " enemies." The food, the warmth, the games shone out all the brighter against the gloomy background of his home. If it hadn't been for Tom and his family he would, indeed, have been wretched.

It was at this point in his reflections that he heard footsteps, and looking up saw Alasdair coming swinging down the road towards him. He had a kind of swaggering walk, one arm held a little out from the body as if to balance him and the other on his stick. Spot ran up to Jim, jumping all over him. Jim was busy examining his heel when Alasdair came abreast. Alasdair, too, looked at it. " Why, boy, you've got a nasty blister there. How did you manage that and you so used to walking? We'd better go to the Grants and get it bathed. No, don't put your stocking on, you might get dye into it and be lame for life." Jim was painfully aware that his feet were dirty from plunging in and out of bogs the day before. He had been so tired he had just rolled into bed the way he was, so now he followed Alasdair reluctantly, keeping his bare foot on the grass verge. If Alasdair had not been waiting for him at Grant's gate he would have fled past, but as it was Alasdair ushered him into the kitchen, saying, " I've brought you a patient, Charlotte. Here's Jim with a sore foot."

The forester looked up from his book. " Hey! I've a bone to pick with you, Alasdair. What were the cattle doing among my young trees? "

" Aye! " said Alasdair with a sad shake to his head. " I thought I'd better come in quick and get it over, though there's the culprit." Here he nodded over to Jim. " Hasn't he brought the cattle up every Sunday for the last nine months, so I never gave them a thought till I saw it was twelve o'clock and still no sign of my herdboy—I was out fishing with George last night."

" You haven't heard about Effie, then? " exclaimed Charlotte, as she brought a basin of warm water for Jim's foot. " She was operated on for acute appendicitis last night—oh! she's doing all right—Charlie met Murdo at the end of the road just now and he told him."

At this news Jim felt as if a great load had fallen off his back. He sat and beamed, not minding how much the disinfectant Mrs. Grant had put in the water stung his sore heel or even when she began to bathe the gashes on his leg.

"My! you have made a mess of yourself, Jim. Whatever have you been doing?" Alasdair put in.

"Of course, you didn't hear it was Jim who fetched the doctor. Was it then you cut yourself?" Jim nodded and told them about the loose barbed wire. Then, of course, the whole story had to be told, not very well, but haltingly in answer to questions showered on him by his listeners.

"So that's why you slept in! And small wonder! Why in the world did you let me fly out at you instead of telling me what you'd been doing?" Alasdair sounded most reproachful.

"You didn't give me a minute——" Jim began and blushed crimson when the Grants laughed heartily.

"I'll bet he didn't, Jim. He jumped down your throat! Time enough for explanations after he came up again!" said the forester, giving Alasdair a quizzical glance.

Alasdair shook his head again at his own errors. "I'm right sorry, Jim, boy, for you're a hero and even Charlie, here, won't have the heart to blame us about the trees now."

Jim felt himself to be in a seventh heaven, his foot made comfortable, and a soothing ointment rubbed to his shoulders. He had never had so much attention in his whole life.

"It was a mercy you reached the doctor in time," Charlotte concluded. "How could Murdo ever manage without Effie? I hope you'll be around when I fall ill for I'm sure you'd go much faster than *his* Baby Austin. I tell you what—you'll both stay to dinner. It's baby's birthday and I've made him a cake and Jim will share it."

The baby sat in his high-chair cooing and gurgling, clattering his spoon on the wooden shelf in front of him. He saw his beautiful pink-iced cake go down Jim's throat without the slightest concern but every now and then he dropped his spoon on the floor so that Jim might pick it up.

All in all it was a wonderful celebration. Jim sat down on the sofa thinking he and Alasdair would soon need to go and see to the cattle but there was no walk for Jim that day. He fell fast asleep where he sat and when Mrs. Grant noticed she put his feet up on the sofa and made him comfortable. Alasdair went off by himself.

"It doesn't seem right," Charlotte said all of a sudden. "I mean the way Alasdair treats Jim—oh! I know it was all a mistake today, but all the same, he always expects Jim to be at his beck and call and why should he be?"

"Well, he wants to be," replied Charlie, glancing up from his book, "so that's all right."

But his wife still looked thoughtful.

"I don't suppose Alasdair will stay very long in Brae, will he? And what will happen to Jim when he goes?"

"Why, he'll be growing up, looking for a job most likely. He'll be all right."

"Alasdair has never stayed very long at anything, has he?"

"Oh! I don't know so much about that. He went to sea to make money and since then he's been droving. He likes moving about a bit but what's wrong with that?"

"Well, he shouldn't treat Jim as if he owned him!" retorted Charlotte with a little spurt of temper. But her husband only laughed.

"I thought you liked Alasdair!"

"Oh! I like him all right—he gets round everyone, I think, but it's too one-sided! Jim thinks the world of him and *he* just makes use of him."

She shook her head, not understanding her own forebodings. Jim slept on, unheeding.

11. *Tug of War*

When Murdo saw Jim later that week he rung his hand so hard that Jim winced, but all he said was, "Thank you, Jim, thank you!"

Tom had to stay off school to look after the little ones and Jim had only glimpses of him till an aunt came to take charge. Jim missed him sorely in school, as he and Bella grappled with sums on compound interest. The sun beat upon the roof and without Tom's aid they sighed a great deal, rubbed out, and began again. The worst of it was that Jim was trying to do his best because Alasdair had pointed out to him how useful arithmetic was to any dealer. "You must have your figures at your fingertips," he kept saying. "When you're buying you have to do sums quick in your head, sums like this one: two hundred and fifty lambs at twenty pounds the clad score, so many shotts to the score." But Miss Menzies, unhappily, didn't notice his unaccustomed efforts or perhaps she thought it was too late.

Miss Menzies came in all smiles one morning and told Donnie that he had won a bursary which would take him to Portree School in the autumn. "And if you work hard, Mary, and you, too, Katie-Ann, you will win bursaries next year." And she smiled briskly upon them. For Bella, Tom, and Jim it was the end of the road and they were all delighted.

Tom came to school soon after that looking very pleased. "Mother's home," he whispered to Jim. "Nanag and Susan didn't know her! They wouldn't go near her—it's because she looks so pale and her hands are white—oh! and she wants you to come in after school, Jim, so be sure and don't forget."

But Jim turned as shy as the little girls and hastened home that evening at a most unusual speed.

At last the term drew to an end. Three days, two days, and then only one day. It was almost too good to be true.

"She won't give us sums to-day," Bella said to Jim as they met on the way to school, "only singing."

"Yes, and poetry, and I can't remember a line."

Bella was willing to offer comfort. "She won't mind on the last day."

"I don't mind if she does!" Jim retorted, assuming his part of hardened sinner. It fell out as Bella had predicted, they recited poetry, they sang all together and one or two sang by themselves, Bella among them, the last day giving her unaccustomed courage. Jim could not remember his poem even when prompted by Tom but the teacher did no more than give an exasperated sigh. They all handed in their school books and just then Miss Menzies saw the postman pass by on his bicycle and went to fetch her mail. A burst of excited chatter filled the room. "No more school!" "No more beastly sums!" "No more strap!" At the word "strap" Jim swung his empty satchel round his head and let it go. It flew upwards and the buckle caught the round white globe of the lamp which had so often hypnotised Jim on long, tedious afternoons. It crashed to the floor in a litter of broken glass. The children screamed and scrambled out of the way, crying, "Oooh! Jim Smith, you'll catch it, see if you don't." At this moment in walked Miss Menzies. "What on earth!" she exclaimed, taking in the scatter of glass, the children perched on desks, Jim's guilty look. "You, as usual, Jim Smith! Of all the clumsy oafs! I can't leave the room for one minute, even on the last day, but you do something stupid. Well! your parents will get the bill and I hope they make you pay for it. Sit down! You will stay behind until you have swept up every bit of glass. Ready, then, children. Stand! Good-bye, boys and girls. A happy holiday!"

"Good-bye, Miss!" they chorused and filed sedately to the door. Once outside they ran, shouting gleefully. Jim could hear them as he fetched the shovel and brush and stooped to sweep up the broken pieces. Miss Menzies sat at her desk and watched him. When he thought he had found every fragment she pointed to yet another under a desk. "Do a thing properly when you are doing it. Make that your motto in life!"

When every morsel was safely on the shovel Jim stood awkwardly wondering whether he was free to go. "Well, Jim, I hope you will try and do your work as a man better than you did as a schoolboy. Good-bye." It was a dry parting. School was over at last and that in itself was happiness enough for a while.

But soon he realised that he was far from free to do what he wanted. He had to take his full share of croft work and he noted that he always got the dullest part of that. He would have liked to be at the fanks when they were shearing the ewes but Finlay and Donald went, leaving him to turn an acre of hay alone with Sarah. He knew Alasdair Bàn gave a hand at the shearing and he felt he was missing all the fun. In that mood he hated the swathes of cut hay waiting to be turned with a hand rake, he hated the bare, steep hill without tree or bush on it behind the croft, he hated the mean corrugated iron house, and the very hens picking and scratching about the door.

After days in the fank Donald would complain to Sarah, "*His* dogs! *His* sheep! *His* cattle! They are always the best! Nobody else ever had anything as good, oh! no! And that dog! He's telling stories about what that dog can do, you would think it was human. I don't believe a word of them, just a pack of blooming lies."

Jim had come in while he was talking and heard the last part of the sentence. "If you mean Alasdair Bàn's dog, it's all true! I've never seen a dog as clever as Glen."

"You've seen a lot of dogs, I must say!" mocked Donald. Sarah listened with a pleased look on her face. Donald was seeing at last what a bad thing it was for the boy to go to Brae and listen to a man like that, filling him up with nonsense, putting ideas into his head! He wanted to be a cattleman, did he? All the cattle he'd ever look after would be their two cows and a few stirks. Sarah pursed her lips. She'd read Donald a lecture at bed-time. He must keep the boy out of Brae! Because Alasdair's tall yarns had so irritated Donald he agreed this time with his wife and kept Jim endlessly busy. If it hadn't been for Sunday Jim would have been quite cut off. The rest of the township looked on at the tug o' war.

"Well! you cannot rightly call it even that!" chuckled old Hugh, Alec John's father. "For Alasdair doesn't pull yet the boy goes to *him* in spite of all three of them heaving on the rope!"

The next phase came when Alasdair suddenly said, "It would be grand if you could come on the road with me to Kyle, you'd be a real help!" They had been passing the cattle under review, a favourite Sunday occupation, putting them into lots as for selling. The animals were sleek and polished, basking in the summer sun, lazily switching their tails to banish horse flies. Gone were the days when they had come running at the sight of man and boy, eager for cake. Now they were independent.

"Go to Kyle!" gasped Jim. If Alasdair had said "China" he could not have been more astonished. "They'd never let me!"

"Och! maybe they would!" replied Alasdair. "It's not like last year. You're well on with the harvest, you've only the one piece of corn to cut and with this weather there's no bother in it."

But Jim felt something akin to irritation. Why should Alasdair raise his hopes so carelessly? For it could never happen.

Donald and Finlay would see to that or, if somehow they were brought round, there was still Sarah and she would always oppose anything Jim wanted. Didn't Alasdair understand what he was up against? Seemingly he didn't for the very next time he saw Donald he broached the subject. This was at the September cattle sales, just a year to the day when he had first come to the place. Alasdair began by praising Donald's bullocks. They were well bred, Alasdair remarked, and well looked after. He hadn't seen anything to beat them in the round of sales he had just attended. He had been in on the bidding for them and succeeded in raising the price on a mainland dealer without being left with them himself. All this put Donald in the best of tempers, his weak face split by a huge grin. Alasdair struck while the iron was hot. Jim, he said, must have got Donald's eye for a good beast, he had had a good training with the two brothers. He would be a great help to them now and so he should be, so he should, but it would be a good thing if he brought home a little

128

money from time to time. Alasdair could make use of him on the road to Kyle to give him a hand with the cattle. He would be three days on the road. Of course, there were other boys in the township, it was true, likely lads, but not one of them had the same eye for cattle. Suppose a beast went lost, one out of forty, he'd back Jim to know which one it was and pick it out even if it got muddled up in another herd. "It's a gift," Alasdair concluded, "just a gift—he must have got it from you, Donald."

Donald nodded his head, hugely delighted. Of course, of course, the boy took it from him. He, Donald, had a sharp eye for a good beast. Hadn't he topped the sale with his pen of bullocks? They had all laughed at him when he took them home last year but they were laughing on the wrong side of their faces now. Alasdair nodded agreement—the decision hung in the balance——

"Aye! to be sure, he gets it from me," Donald maundered

on. " Well, if he'll be of use to you I'm sure he can go as far as the ferry."

" Well! that's grand!" cried Alasdair heartily. " You're a real neighbour, Donald. There's not a boy in the place would suit me so well but just the one you trained." On this the two of them went off together in great good spirits towards the distillery—Finlay was already ahead—after telling Jim to look after Alasdair's new lot of cattle.

Jim, with Tom to help him, got them on the move. Once they had them plodding gently up the hill Jim had time to tell Tom the news.

" He'll let me go as far as Kyle, Tom! I never *dreamt* he'd let me but Alasdair buttered him up saying how well he taught me. Taught me!" Jim stood still in the middle of the road to laugh at that. " He never taught me a thing! It's only this last year since I've been going up to Brae that I learnt to use my eyes."

" Well, it's grand he's letting you go," said Tom. " Will you be long on the road?"

" Three days!" replied Jim, all aglow at the very thought, and for a moment he looked down on Tom who wasn't going to go anywhere and would probably be making cornstacks when he, Jim, was off on an adventure.

They stopped for a breather on the crest of the hill. The blue of the sky was masked by fleecy white clouds, men on the far side of the loch were busy in their fields, the flowers of the heather were now fading but the moor grass was turning russet and bronze.

" It's not like the day we had a year ago!" remarked Tom. " You'd hardly believe it was the same place."

" That's the day we first met Alasdair and he took us to the Martins' house—remember how the old man tried to hit the auctioneer!——but the daughter gave us a grand feed. Pity we hadn't time to go to-day! Goodness! We still had a year to do at school!" Jim took a deep breath. It was hard to put into words what he felt. From where they stood they could see hill upon hill away into the blue distance. So for a moment he thought of his life, opening into unexpected possibilities. He would soon stand on this very road, the herd ahead of him, Alasdair Bàn and the dogs for company, new places, new people ahead!

All he said was, " Come on, Tom! I'll have to put this lot right over to the cliffs. We'd better get a move on."

Donald Bruce told Sarah that very night of his decision. If he had not told her then he would have lacked the courage to come out with it in the cold light of morning. Once he had broken the news he stuck manfully to his word in spite of disapproval which was silent to begin with but then declared itself in a furious tirade. " You're soft! " she hissed at him. " Just soft! He'll get him away from us—isn't that what he's working for? Isn't that how it is already? Does he ever stay at home if he can be up at Brae? Does he? Does he? And now you're letting him go to Kyle! Have you taken leave of your senses? "

Donald shifted uncomfortably in his chair. He hated standing up to Sarah but this time he had given his word and couldn't go back on it.

" The boy's going! " he shouted loudly to keep up his courage. " See and have a clean shift ready for him that he won't disgrace us among strangers. Iron him a shirt! "

" He hasn't got a shirt."

" Well, it's about time he had! I'll go over to the shop and get him one, for I won't have them saying we can't afford the lad a shirt."

Sarah looked at him and the air was thick with all the things she didn't say, but Finlay muttered, " A shirt? I never had a shirt at his age. Humph! what's the world coming to? When I got a shirt I earned it."

Donald vented his annoyance on his brother. " Well! he's

earned it, too. Who tramped the stack for you and who carried the thatch and stood by to hand it up to you or you wouldn't be finished yet, sitting down every half hour for a smoke?"

Finlay was so startled by this sudden attack that the pipe fell out of his hand and the bowl broke. "Oh! *gu siorruidh*! my pipe," he murmured, "my good pipe, the best pipe I ever had and now it's broken."

Once roused Donald was as good as his word and walked over to the village shop the very next day and bought a striped flannel shirt. Stroking it with his rough hand he felt immensely proud of his purchase. The shopman, taking advantage of his customer's mood, laid out on the counter next to the jars of sweets some ties, a black, a blue, and a green. Donald admired them very much and saw that the blue one would go with the blue stripe in the shirt so he bought it. While the man was making up his parcel he gazed round the tightly packed little shop, at the stand of picture postcards, the walking sticks, the loaves of bread, kegs of salt herring, and hanging overhead pair upon pair of heavy hill boots, made of horsehide. He banged his fist on the wooden counter. That was it! He knew the boy needed something else, and that was it! A pair of boots! Size seven, he told the man with pride, the boy was big for his age being just fourteen. Laden with his parcels he reached home in the evening and at once made Jim try on the shirt. Jim was bashful and would have preferred to try it on alone in his bedroom. He pleaded that he was dirty but Donald only hustled him out to the burn to wash and when he came back he himself put the shirt over Jim's head.

"There!" he said, standing back to admire the effect. "Doesn't he look well?"

Sarah was sitting as usual by the fire. She mutely refused to turn her head or look at Jim. If she could only have joined in, Jim suddenly thought, and been proud of him what a difference it would have made, but the chance slipped by.

" Try on the boots! " Donald ordered, but flatly, as if the bounce had gone out of him. Jim tried them on. They looked grand but in a short time he was complaining of the right foot hurting him. Donald was quite annoyed. He told Jim to keep wearing them for the last few days to " break them in " but in the end it was plain that Jim's feet would break sooner. When he was convinced of this his foster-father made Finlay patch up the old pair for him. He, himself, cut Jim's hair and even brushed his suit when Sarah refused to do anything at all. The tension in the house grew so strong that Jim found he could hardly eat and his sleep was once more troubled with dreams. Tom arrived shortly before he left with a gaberdine coat of his own on his arm.

" Och! I won't need that! " protested Jim. " It's too warm."

" You're to take it, Mum says. The weather could turn cold any time."

" Right, Tom, thanks."

It came as a tremendous relief next day when Donald told him to get ready. He was to go up to Brae that afternoon to lend a hand collecting the beasts. He could still hardly credit that Sarah would let him go. But he washed, he rubbed himself so hard his ears shone like lanterns, he put on the new shirt, and tied the new tie, and still she sat sullenly in her chair and said not a word. He took a stick, put the coat over his arm.

" You'll do! " declared Donald.

At that he was out of the door and on to the road like a stirk getting out of a byre in spring. Excitement bubbled up in him but responsibility acted as a check. He had to drive towards Brae all the cattle on Grasco, leave them at the Corry Mor burn, and then drive the cows which were not to be sold, with their calves, right up into the Corry Mor out of sight of the rest. Alasdair had the cattle to gather on his side and the " winterers " —the cattle he meant to keep all winter—had to be put far over out of the way also.

It was already growing dark when Jim got back from the

Corry Mor but he could just make out Alasdair coming along with his herd and he could very easily hear them, bellowing at being disturbed from their usual pastures.

Jim sighed with delight when he sat down to a supper of salmon (" And don't ask where that came from! "). The small room glowed in the lamplight. Spot sat by his side, eyes fixed on every mouthful. Jim slipped him a piece of bread.

" Give the dogs the scraps along with their porridge," said Alasdair, " and when you've washed up make for your bed."

" Och! it's too early." Jim wanted to sit and hear Alasdair's yarns by the fire.

But Alasdair was firm. " We've got to be up long before daylight and we've a long day after that."

For a while Jim lay awake, seeing the sliver of lamplight below the door but long before Alasdair smoored the fire for the night he had fallen fast asleep.

12. On the Road

"Jim, wake up!" Alasdair was shaking him by the shoulder. "Jim! you'd do for one of the seven sleepers! Up you get, now. I'll have a cup of tea ready for you so put your clothes on quick."

Still half asleep Jim tumbled out of bed, dressed in his new shirt, and made a poor job of tying the new blue tie by candle-light. When he went into the kitchen Alasdair was pouring tea into a mug.

"Drink that, it'll wake you up, and take a piece—we've no time for a proper breakfast. We must catch the cattle before they move."

Jim did as he was told, watching the flames flicker in the grate as he chewed at a hunk of bread and cheese. The whole thing felt unreal as if it was one of his dreams. Soon he'd wake up beside Finlay. The house looked sad and abandoned as houses do when their tenants leave them. They had no time to tidy up but left the bed unmade, the scraps of their last meal on the table. Alasdair carefully raked out the fire. "Put your coat on," he told Jim, "it's sharp." The dogs, each in his own way, were eager to be off. Glen gave one joyous bark and then went to his master's heel, Spot kept up a volley of barks till told to stop. The air struck cold, the stars were shining, the land was black, but the sky was paling. They walked round the bay above the shore and crossed the plank bridge over the stream. Even so close as that they could scarcely make out the cattle though there were almost fifty lying near.

"You go round that side, Jim, I'll go this, and we'll get them

135

on their feet. When they're all up we'll count them to be sure we have the lot."

"I make it forty-two," said Jim.

"Forty-three," said Alasdair. "Try again."

This time they both made it forty-three but there had been forty-five the night before.

"Pity if we have to leave two behind. Can you think which two it is, Jim?"

"There was a roan-coloured heifer trying to follow the cows last night but I turned her back."

"Maybe she went after them again and took another with her. Take a run up, it might be worth it, but if they're not there, don't worry, just come straight on and if I find them ahead of me I'll whistle."

Jim zigzagged up the brae, calling to Spot. He reached the corry to find it still twilight and hurried impatiently from one old ruin to another vainly seeking the cows. Then he saw the white one a little ahead of him with her calf, now grown big, lying beside her. She turned mildly curious eyes upon him as he passed. Other cows rose first on their hind legs, then on their fore, stretching each way, their calves running in to suckle. But still no heifers! Burning with impatience and imagining the herd already past Udale he promised himself that he would turn back if he had no luck at the next green dyke but looking down from the top of it he saw the missing heifer and a blue-grey she had enticed away with her. Spot and he had them quickly on the move. He looked behind him once to make sure he wasn't being followed but the cows were grazing peacefully, content to be left alone with their calves. At that moment the rim of the sun came over the black line of the hill. To the boy it was a good omen and with a light heart he hastened after the herd.

That first day his spirits mounted with every step they took out of the glen, with every step that took him away from his everyday world. They walked slowly, at two miles an hour, and, climbing the hill, Jim's only regret was that there was no one awake to admire them.

It was a beautiful autumn day, the moor wine-red and the hills softly blue and hazy. The sun shone as if it were midsummer and Jim wished he had never taken Tom's coat, but Alasdair assured him he'd be glad enough of it before he got home.

" The weather can change pretty quick at this time of year." They proceeded for another half-mile and then Alasdair asked was he hungry. Jim nodded. He was so hungry he'd been regretting not putting a piece of bread in his pocket. He had begun to wonder whether, like the cattle, they were to go all day without food. The beasts, indeed, helped themselves as they went along and he had been envying them when the drover spoke.

" I'm sure you are! Well, we'll put the cattle in the lodge park. The shooting tenants are gone and the gamekeeper is a friend of mine, then we'll see if Mary has anything for us to-day. You mind Mary? She gave us a meal once before."

Did Jim remember? Of course he did, he would never forget that autumn sale in the storm, the cosy little house, and the nice, cheerful woman. All he said was, " I mind."

" Aye, well, we could do with something inside us now. That's a nice firm fence," Alasdair remarked, giving the strainer a shake, "and all to keep in two ponies, but it'll do us a good turn to-day for we can take our meal in peace."

They re-crossed the bridge and made for the Martins' cottage. The door opened before they could knock and old John welcomed them in. " We've got the kettle on," he chirped, " we saw you coming, but that silly girl of mine is trying to keep a kitten alive."

They found Mary on her knees trying to slip spoonfuls of milk into a kitten's mouth. She looked up and smiled at them. " Poor thing, its mother must have been caught in a trap."

Alasdair cast an eye on it. " You'd be as well to drown it. You'll never keep it alive."

" And why should she keep it alive? I'm sure if we've one cat about the place we've a dozen waifs and strays."

Mary put the kitten in a basket near the fire and got to her feet.

" You'd better look after us, Mary," smiled Alasdair. " I've a lad with me who's as hungry as the kitten." This made Mary look at Jim.

" Why!" she exclaimed. " Isn't this one of the boys you had with you last year, Alasdair? My! but he's grown and filled out, too. I'd hardly have known him. He'll be taller than yourself soon."

" He will not!" retorted Alasdair, who was jealous of his inches, then seeing Jim's crestfallen look, he added, " But he'll do well enough!"

" Is that all you can say?" cried Mary with a toss of her head—she was busy laying a white cloth on the table. " I bet he has you run off your feet while he strolls along giving the orders. Oh! I knew him when he was at school and a lazy scholar he was! If he could get someone else to do his sums for him——" she broke out laughing at Jim's incredulous look. " No doubt he was telling you to work hard, eh? To be sure! I thought so!"

" That will do!" replied Alasdair indignantly. " I was first in my class, she was just plain jealous and what are you doing with that cloth? It's not the gentry you're going to entertain!"

" I like a white cloth. Likely you have a bare table yourself!"

" No table's bare with good food on it!"

" Oh! so you fancy yourself as a cook, now?"

" I've got someone with me who'll tell you what a good cook I am!" But Jim was too bashful to join in the conversation.

" Away!" Mary laughed. " He's that scared of you—and I don't blame him. He wouldn't dare tell the truth but wait till I get him alone—och! he's blushing as red as a beet. It's the lies you're making him tell, Alasdair!"

"Can you not be quiet, girl," her father rebuked her. "Get the pan on the fire! I got a wedder last week, been up in the Coolins for years. It had three fleeces on it."

"And fat!" Mary joined in as she cut thin slices of black pudding. "You wouldn't believe how fat that beast was and coming off bare rocks."

The smell as the slices cooked on the pan made Jim's mouth water. It felt an age to him before Mary dished them on hot plates and told them to draw in their chairs. Jim polished off three slices with fried eggs as well and he didn't refuse a fourth slice when Mary pressed it on him.

"Well, you should do, boy," Alasdair remarked. "You could reach Kyle on what you've eaten, let alone going no farther than Sligachan to-night."

"Let the boy be, Alasdair, we could eat whales when we were his age!"

The men lit their pipes, smoked, and gossiped. "Are you going all the way to Dingwall?" Mary asked Jim as she stacked the dishes. He shook his head regretfully. "Och! well, you'll see the ferry, and the trains, and the railway line. There's not much to Dingwall, after all, but the one long street and the cattle market."

She didn't realise that *that* was the very thing he wanted most to see. Still, apart from that, she was so kind that Jim was almost sorry to leave. She began buttering a piece to put in his pocket though Alasdair told her they'd be fed like kings in the hotel. "It'll do no harm in your pocket!" said Mary. "Wait!" She went into the closet to return a moment later with a big blue handkerchief with a red border. She put it into Jim's breast pocket, saying, "It's one my brother Lachie left the last time he was home from sea. There! It suits you grand. Off you go and good luck to you!"

The men had already reached the park and the dogs were bringing the beasts out of the gate, old John examining each one

as it passed. Jim stood near the bridge in case any should have a mind to bolt homewards. He stood with both hands on the crook of his long stick just as Alasdair always did.

"Well, you've got some grand animals there, Alasdair!" was old John's verdict as he wished them a good journey.

The road went first through a wide, green glen but before night they had left the green places behind and were crossing a rough moor, strewn with boulders. Towards sundown they descended the long hill above the inn. Here there was no park but Alasdair drove the herd across the humpbacked bridge and a short distance off the road. "They're tired," he commented. "I don't think they'll try to move to-night."

Jim was looking about him in surprise. Here was just this

one, long, white building set among these savage-looking hills,
all rocks and pinnacles. It was almost like a foreign country—
it was so unlike home. He stepped down to the river to wash his
face and hands and noticed that the water ran clear over the
blue-grey pebbles. This made it quite unlike the peat-coloured
water he had always known.

Alasdair was still watching the herd, some of which were
drinking, others had already lain down.

"This was a great place in the old days," he said. "They held
the cattle market here in May. You'd get cattle coming from all
over Skye, aye! and from Uist and Harris as well. You'd see
crofters with only one or two stirks and drovers with big herds.
The whole place would be full of them bargaining and hoping

for enough money to buy meal for the winter. Well! I think they're going to settle all right. I'll take a look out again before I go to bed. Come on, Jim."

Alasdair took him past the main door of the hotel and entered one at the side. He led the way down a long passage, opened a door at the far end, and the noise which they had heard as they approached suddenly ceased, then broke out afresh.

There were cries of "Well! Alasdair, where have you been hiding yourself?" The stout cook said she had been growing thin pining for a sight of him, and the pretty waitresses declared they were all going into a decline. A boy, not much older than Jim, sat strumming a ukelele and smiling quietly at all the carry-on.

"What sort of a thing is that?" asked Alasdair with obvious disapproval. "You should be playing the pipes!"

"Lord save us from the pipes!" Mary-Ann, the cook, exclaimed. "They'd bring the boss on top of us. Oh! yes, there's one or two of those mad climbers about yet but we'll be shutting up soon and going off home and I won't be sorry. I'm tired to death. Ishbel! bring the cold roast. Katie! set the table like a good girl. When you've had your supper, Bessie will sing you a song and you'll hear how well Alec can play that thing. Now! let's hear all your news, Alasdair."

While the cook and Alasdair settled down to a good crack Jim sat silent, too shy to distinguish between Ishbel and Bessie, Chrissie and Kate, but when supper came he wasn't backward in tackling his huge portion of roast beef, but he wouldn't try any of the sauces out of bottles which Alasdair urged upon him. Chutneys and beetroot were too much of a novelty but the trifle which the girls heaped on his plate was the best thing he had ever tasted. Chrissie kept giving him more till Alasdair noticed what was happening and put a stop to it. "You'll make the laddie sick!" he protested. "And what will I do then? I'd have to take you along to Kyle with me, Mary-Ann."

" You'd have to carry me on your back, then ! " laughed the cook, all her chins shaking with merriment.

" Mary-Ann, it would be a pleasure ! " Everyone in the kitchen rocked with laughter at the thought till Mary-Ann said, " That's enough of your nonsense, Alasdair Bàn ! Bessie will give us a song now." Which Bessie did after much giggling and many requests. She had a pure, sweet voice and the song made Jim both happy and sad at the same time which surprised him. He watched Alasdair enjoying himself mightily in all the company and thought how lucky he was to be with him. Once started the girls went from song to song, people drifted in to enjoy the *ceilidh*, and to add their own songs and stories. But all too soon Jim was ordered off to bed. Bessie showed him up to a little room above the scullery. He crawled over to the far side of the big double bed feeling the sheets cold. For a short time he was aware of sounds coming up from below but long before Alasdair had finished yarning and taken a last look at the cattle he was fast asleep, tired out by his long day on the road.

Next morning, from the warmth of the hotel kitchen, he stepped into a strange, cold world, a landscape of the moon, hills rising almost vertical from sea level, swept bare of soil—skeleton hills. This weird, desolate scene was lit by the pale gleams of the waning moon.

They had three miles of narrow road ahead of them, the loch on one side and steep hill on the other. Alasdair was in a hurry to get through this before traffic came on them and scattered the beasts. At the end of this stretch they turned off the main road, taking the old road up the hill.

" We can take our time now," said Alasdair, " no cars to bother us here. This was the way the drovers used to go after buying their cattle, like I was telling you last night, at the Sligachan Fair. They'd walk as far as Falkirk and Stirling, aye, and even on into England. You wouldn't want to walk as far as that, eh, Jim ? "

"I'd like it fine," Jim said.

"Och! well, it's all right in good weather like to-day (the sun had risen by this time and changed the morning cold to a pleasant warmth) but in mist and rain and sleeping out as they did, it wouldn't be so good. Seemingly there was a great trade in cattle away back, black cattle, they called them, but a student was telling me they weren't like the Aberdeen-Angus we have here, no, they were dun-coloured, he thought, and very much smaller and lighter. So you see, the glens in Skye were well known for raising good beasts. Aye! and another thing—you could give me the date of the battle of Culloden?"

"Seventeen forty-six," said Jim promptly.

"Aye! I thought you could. We always had that date drummed into us. Well! the drovers were walking up this road that year like any other year for people must trade and eat, no matter who's fighting."

"Did they meet the redcoats?"

"I don't suppose they saw a redcoat or a clansman either," said Alasdair. "There, Jim, we're at the top of the pass. We're in Lord Macdonald's deer forest." All round them were the dark, grim hills, their tops bare of soil. No houses were to be seen, only the sea below them, the tide far out, exposing a great stretch of brown seaweed. Tiny figures were bent double at the water's edge.

"Picking whelks for the London market," explained the drover. "A slow job and a cold one. If the whelks were in Udale, Donald would have had you picking them! You were lucky."

They climbed downwards, crossing stream after stream, till they rounded the loch. Jim began to long for the sight of a house. Here it was all moor, not a sound but the lap of the waves or the gurgle of a burn.

"When we get round the next bend," Alasdair said cheerfully, breaking in on Jim's thoughts, "we'll push the cattle up another stretch of old road and we'll visit an old friend of mine. Mairead Og will give us a big welcome."

Mairead Og! (Young Margaret). Jim at once pictured a nice, plump young woman like Mary Martin, and he looked forward to their visit.

" There's the house! " said Alasdair, pointing to a small cottage right beside the shore. It had a rowan tree at the back and three small coils of hay covered in fishnet in the yard. The dogs drove the cattle off the road and then Alasdair led the way round the thatched cottage, his tackety boots ringing out on the cobble stones. A very old woman came out, saying, " Who's there? " in a thin, high voice.

" Alasdair Bàn—— " the drover began, but she interrupted him, her little nutcracker face lighting up.

" Is it yourself, Alasdair, my darling? Was I not keeping an eye for you these last few days for I knew you wouldn't pass an old friend—— "

" And no more I would," replied Alasdair. " I never pass old friends and I have brought a young friend to see you. This is Jim."

The old woman kept his hand in her old dry one while she scrutinised him keenly, much to Jim's embarrassment. " He's not like you, Alasdair! " she pronounced, finally.

" Oh! he's not related to me," explained Alasdair. " He's just giving me a hand on the road."

This point cleared up to the old lady's satisfaction she led them into her little house, but she had forgotten about her dog. As soon as it saw Spot it fell upon him in a most ferocious manner. Pandemonium reigned, Alasdair shouting, Mairead shrieking, dogs snapping, snarling, growling, and yelping, till Mairead seized a bucket of water and emptied it over the pair of them.

" Ow! " came from Jim as water sloshed into his boot. " Ow! " from the dogs as Alasdair dragged Spot outside and Mairead pushed and pulled her dog, water pouring from his shaggy coat, into a closet. Glen, like the wise dog he was, had been all the time under a wooden settle, and Jim wished heartily he had been along with him.

Alasdair came back in, exclaiming, "The rascal! I gave him a wallop. That'll learn him. Oh! dear, we've made a terrible mess of the house for you! Give Jim a pail and a cloth and he'll dry up the water."

Of all the stupid houses this was the stupidest! Jim thought crossly, as he tried to mop up what felt like Loch Lomond in the middle of the kitchen floor. First of all you had an old woman called "young" and then there was Alasdair being as nice to her as he had been to the pretty girls in Sligachan and she was going on about having no ham in the house, she hadn't been to the shop that week, though if she'd known they were coming she'd have bought a whole pound—and so on, and so on. If only she'd stop nattering and cook something, anything! I'll pass out, he thought, wringing out the cloth into the pail for the twentieth time, that'll be the next thing. His temper was not improved by Alasdair telling him to put some vim into the job and showing him how to wring the cloth till not a drop of water was left in it. At last, however, Mairead had food on the table, even though it was only boiled eggs.

"You'll have to do with what the old crone has!" she cackled, smiting Jim a blow on the shoulder which made him wince. "Why, he's blushing like a girl! You're hungry? That's the best sauce! And isn't it lucky, now, I churned yesterday—it'll be the last time till she calves in spring."

"Is she going dry already, and not calving till spring?" asked Alasdair. "That's too long. I'll find you a young cow that won't go dry till a month before calving."

But Mairead, sitting in the basket chair by the fire, shook her head. "What would I do with a young beast? Susan and I are well suited. She's like myself, she's seen all the ills of this world, and now she's waiting for the end."

146

This made Alasdair look serious. "You shouldn't be all alone, Mairead, it's not good for you."

She gave a cackle of laughter. "Who said I was alone? Calum Mor, that's my neighbour, Jim, comes in every night and tells me all his troubles, the rheumatics he has and the pains in his chest and one eye not seeing the same as the other and spasms in his stomach and dear knows what else. Well! I cheer him up as best I can but, oh! how glad I am when I can turn him out of the house at midnight and have my aches and pains to myself."

Alasdair laughed with her. "I wasn't going to give you to an old dodderer like Calum Mor!" he protested.

"No, indeed, I would hope not! It's yourself I was considering, Alasdair."

"And it's myself you would get, too, Mairead, if I'd just had the luck to be born a few years earlier." This reply delighted her so much that she laughed till she cried. What a way for an old woman to behave! Talking about marriage! She should leave things like that to young, well-favoured people and not make a fool of herself. It wasn't decent!

Jim ate in sulky silence while the two of them talked of old days and of people they had both known and of distant relatives. That was a subject Jim hated. Without a single relative of his own such talk made him feel left out. He was glad when Alasdair told him to go out and see that the cattle were all right. He left hurriedly, not saying either "thank you" or "good-bye." Spot, who had been waiting patiently at the door, jumped up on him, his wet paws resting on Jim's shoulders, but Jim was so pleased to be clear of the house he fondled him and the two of them raced up the hill to where the herd was quietly grazing. They sat on a bank together, waiting for Alasdair.

At last he came along, swinging his stick. "She's a grand old woman, that one," were his first words. Jim had hoped to hear no more of Mairead Og.

" Why do they call her ' og ' when she's so old ? " he asked, glumly.

" The name just stuck, I suppose. She married young but her husband was lost at sea, so she brought up the family herself. The youngest was born after his father died."

" It sounds silly for an old woman to be called young."

Alasdair stopped short and gave him a cold stare. " You think so, do you? Well, let me tell you this, she's as young as anyone I know. She has a memory that puts my own to shame."

Jim would have been wise to say no more but his disappointment bubbled up. " She made such a fuss about the food and then it was only boiled eggs ! "

The words had no sooner left his mouth than he regretted them, but it was too late. Alasdair turned on him in sudden fury, his blue eyes sparkling with anger.

" If you want to walk the roads with me, don't let me hear you say a thing like that ! She gave us what she had—it was the best she had and she gave it with a good heart, and you ! What did you do ? You had a sulky look on your face the whole time you were in and then you walked out of the door without even saying ' thank you.' Anyone who walks the roads with me will have to learn better manners than that ! "

The colour rose in Jim's cheeks. He found nothing to say and fell a pace or two behind. In heavy silence they walked close by the sea and then between birch trees spilling their small red and yellow leaves over the road, but shortly after that Alasdair began to whistle—the storm was past—and to the tune of " The Barren Rocks of Aden " they came into Broadford in the evening.

13. *The Railway Journey*

They stayed that night with second cousins of Alasdair's on his mother's side but Jim was too tired to sort them out. He ate the evening meal in a haze of fatigue and shortly afterwards was taken up to a huge double bed with brass knobs which twinkled in the light of the small red lamp. So many different people, so many strange houses and new beds! What a lot he would have to tell Tom when he got home though he wouldn't tell him about the quarrel. He'd just say she was a funny old woman.

It was bitterly cold in the morning; Jim's teeth were chattering in spite of the warmth of Tom's gaberdine coat. The waning moon gleamed on hoar-frosted grass, walls, and roofs. The cattle were lying close by the hedge in the big field, the breath steaming from their nostrils, their backs rimed with the frost. Urged on by the men and dogs they got reluctantly to their feet and were driven through the gate and across the bridge. The village, strung along the main road, was still fast asleep. Here and there a dog barked as they passed, wondering what animals were on the move so early in the dark. The east wind blew strongly in their faces and as they had to walk slowly for the sake of the beasts it was hard to warm up.

"Eight miles to go," mused Alasdair. "That'll take us about three hours. We'll be at the ferry shortly after nine. That will be just right for I like getting into Dingwall in good time to get the beasts on to a good park. Well, you've been a great help, Jim, and I'll be missing you."

" Can I cross the ferry? "

" Surely! " said Alasdair. " The bus doesn't go till three in the afternoon. You'll have all day to fill in."

They were crossing a bleak moor, having left the high hills behind, but the sea was still close on their left. Ahead lay more high hills but these, Alasdair told him, were on the mainland. On that first journey Jim became quite confused between what was a part of Skye and what was an island and Alasdair kept putting him right and adding, " You should know your geography."

They reached a point on the road where they could look down on to the village of Kyleakin, and across the narrows to Kyle of Lochalsh. The sea ran south into a tangle of hills.

" There's the pier," said Alasdair, pointing, " and the railway's on it, too."

Jim's eye caught a puff of smoke. " Is the train away? " he asked.

Alasdair smiled. " There's plenty of trains. There'll be one for us, don't you worry. We'll not stop for food on this side till we ferry the cattle then we can enjoy a meal in peace."

The sight of the lighthouse with the small white cottages behind it pleased Jim very much. Drifters were sailing north and a small coal puffer belched a column of black smoke. The village consisted of a row of white, well-tended houses, with the village green in front, between them and the rocky shore.

" Stay here, Jim, till I see if the ferry boat's in. They're better waiting here than on the quay. I won't be a minute."

Small boys sprang up from nowhere, deeply curious. An English visitor came out of the hotel and seeing the shaggy highland cattle cried to her husband to come and see them. " What a chance for a photo! " They had taken several photographs by the time Alasdair came back.

" Get them under way, Jim, the ferry's just coming in, we won't have to wait. She'll take about twenty-two. We can shed the rest at the top of the quay. Now, we'll take it easy. Don't rush them, whatever you do. The tide's low and the jetty's a wee bit slippery."

The first of the cattle nosed their way forward, blowing through their nostrils at this strange road. When these grew afraid and tried to stop they were prevented by the others coming on behind. The ferrymen held a shutter between them and the sea. The only way open to them led on to the boat. Four big bullocks went abreast on to the turntable and more and more pressed on behind. Jim already had his orders to keep the rest at the top of the quay. There they snorted, stamped, tossed their heads, and sometimes jabbed a neighbour with a sharp horn. The loading down at the boat was going like clockwork. "Never seen them easier," said the ferryman as he swung the turntable round. The ferry chugged away across the Kyle.

Left to himself Jim leant on his long stick as the drovers did. Small boys hovered near but he ignored them. Spot, on the other hand, wagged his tail to any stranger in a way totally without dignity. But Spot never had any dignity, only an ever-empty stomach.

"Where are you taking them?" one urchin asked.

"To Dingwall," Jim briefly replied.

"There's no price for cattle these days," said an older boy, evidently quoting a grown-up.

"There'll be a price for those!" retorted Jim and turned his back on them. The animals, meanwhile, were milling around and working themselves up into a state of excitement. It wasn't going to be so easy to get this lot on board, specially when cars, brought over by the ferry on its return journey, passed noisily by them, frightening them still further.

"Right, Jim, bring them down!" Alasdair shouted. Jim moved them slowly on, giving them plenty of time to negotiate the slippery stones at their leisure.

"That's right! That's the style!" said Alasdair approvingly.

" We're going to be lucky with this lot, too." But he spoke too soon. The leaders, certainly, stepped quietly on to the turntable, but then there came a rush. Several of the big Aberdeen-Angus pushed their way on together and the beast on the outside was jostled, lost her footing, teetered on the edge of the slipway, and then fell with a resounding splash into the sea, sending up a huge column of spray. Alasdair swore and so did the ferrymen. The heifer, terror struck, swam round in circles and then made for the shore. Alasdair hurried up the jetty to be ahead of her, Glen at his heels.

" Put the rest on!" the ferryman shouted to Jim who was watching Alasdair and forgetting the business in hand. He drove them on board without further trouble and by the time he was free to look Alasdair was already coming back down the jetty driving the heifer in front of him. Water was running off her coat in streams. She stopped short, shook herself, tossed her head from side to side, showing the whites of her eyes. The village boys closed in behind Alasdair to prevent a breakaway. Alasdair moved at a snail's pace giving her time to settle down. The cattle already on board bellowed to her and she replied. She was still trembling with fright and with cold. " Keep clear!" Alasdair commanded. The ferrymen and Jim retreated farther down the jetty till the waves broke at their feet. The watchers held their breath. She had her forefeet on the plank but again she stopped, sniffing the air and scenting danger. " Give her time! Give her time!" There was a moment's breathless hush, the heifer put one foot forward, all might have been well if one of the village dogs had not escaped from its young master's clutch and sunk its teeth in the heifer's tail. In a flash she swung round, at the same instant Alasdair sprang to catch her horn to keep her by sheer force, but the maddened creature charged straight at him, knocking him over, so that the back of his head hit the causeway. He lay still. The heifer, head down, charged through the village boys scattering them like dust and disappeared from sight round the corner. It had all happened so quickly that Jim had the odd idea that it couldn't really have happened at all. He ran to where Alasdair lay, calling his name. Sandy MacInnes, the ferryman, joined him. " He's knocked out," he said. That was no help.

" What can we do ? " Jim cried. " Oh ! do bring him round."

" Likely he'll come round himself in a wee while—it was just the knock, aye ! and there's a cut, small wonder, and it's bleeding. Well, we can't leave him lying here. Hie ! Alec, run home as fast as you can and tell Tam and Simon to come at once and give us a hand lifting him. Tell your mother to phone the doctor from the post office. Quick, now ! "

The boy darted off and Sandy turned to his brother, John, the other ferryman. " Get my oilskin ! It'll do to cover him till they come. My word, there's a bite in the wind this morning."

Jim shivered as he knelt beside his friend. Only yesterday they had walked in the sunshine together, now the sky was over-cast and Jim was alone, but he was sure the drover would come round at any minute and start ordering everyone about as was his wont, but they covered him with the yellow oilskin and still he did not stir.

" Pulse is all right," Sandy muttered.

" A lorry and two cars waiting on the other side ! " John said. " We'll have to cross soon for the bus will be here any minute."

" Who's to look after the cattle now ? " Sandy asked.

" Well, they can't stay on the boat, that's certain," rejoined the other.

Sandy shook the boy by the shoulder. "What will we do with the cattle ? "

Jim stared first at him and then at Alasdair as if expecting him to answer. But the figure under the oilskin lay inert.

" What will we do ? " the ferryman repeated. " Make up your mind, boy."

Jim shook his head in utter bewilderment. What were they

asking *him* for? He'd never taken any decisions, he had no idea what to do, Alasdair had always arranged everything.

"Here they are!" cried Sandy with relief. Four men were coming down the jetty carrying a door between them. This they placed beside the unconscious man and then lifted him as gently as they could on to the improvised stretcher.

One at each corner, the men lifted the door, grunting a little, then walked as carefully as they could on the uneven stones. People came out of their cars, gazing curiously at the shuffling group. Jim was following blindly, the sight of Alasdair laid like a dead body on a stretcher had terrified him more than anything else in the whole unlucky episode, but Sandy stopped him.

"Look, boy, you can't do him any good now except by looking after his cattle. Take this lot across and they'll help you to put them on the train. The wagons are waiting there for them. Once you get them to Dingwall the yardmen will see that they're all right. He'll come round himself long before saleday. It's just a wee crack he got—what's that to a strong man like Alasdair Bàn? But if you let the cattle go he'll be right annoyed."

What the man said was true. He *must* go on, like it or not.

"What about the heifer?" he asked, suddenly remembering the cause of all their troubles.

"Oh! be damned to the brute," said Sandy. "She'll be all right—I'll tell the police."

With an effort Jim stopped following the little band and was just going to board the ferry when he heard a dog howl. He looked back and saw Glen a little apart sitting on his haunches. The dog raised its muzzle in the air and howled again, an eerie, uncanny sound coming at that moment but it served to remind Jim of Spot. He *must* have a dog.

"Wait!" he called to Sandy. "I'm going for the dog." He ran up the quay, frantically whistling and calling. Once on the road he spied Spot a little farther on outside a small butcher's shop. Jim coaxed and called but Spot only crouched and made no effort to go to him. With his hand outstretched Jim drew closer. " Spot! Come on, Spot! There's a good dog." With a quick movement he seized him by the scruff of the neck, lifted him bodily, and ran back to the waiting ferry.

Sandy helped him on board and gave him a length of cord to tie round Spot's neck. By the time he looked back the boat was more than half-way over. The men carrying Alasdair were out of sight but still over the beat of the engine he heard Glen's dismal lament. For two pins he could have howled himself. Here he was—in charge of forty-four animals, without the least idea how he was to get them to Dingwall nor what he was to do with them when, or if, he got there. It was like a nightmare, worse, because he couldn't wake up and say, " Oh! it was only a dream."

But to begin with things went reasonably well. The cattle walked sedately off the ferry and up the slipway. The station was easy to find and two porters helped him pen the cattle alongside the rest. " We'll be trucking them about eleven," one of the porters told Jim, " so you'll have time for a bite of food. There's a nice wee place at the corner and they're not dear."

It was then, listening to the helpful porter, that Jim realised the depth of his plight. He had no money! Alasdair would have given him money for the return journey but the accident prevented that. He was already hungry, very hungry, indeed.

They had had a bite at four in the morning. It felt to him as if six days had passed since then, not six hours. And what about a ticket? He knew you had to buy a ticket when you travelled on a train. Well, he couldn't buy a ticket. His mind in a turmoil he crossed the railway bridge and found himself outside the tea-shop. A group of travellers just off the ferry were outside. " Time for a nice cup of tea before the train," he heard one man say, and they all trooped in, laughing and joking. Jim's heart was sore. Every one of that lot would have had a nice warm breakfast that morning already and there they were enjoying cups of tea and buns.

He loitered down a side road and found himself back on the pier. High cattle trucks stood waiting. One of MacBrayne's steamers, its red funnel topped by a black line, was just casting off with people on board waving to those on the pier. He sat down on a bollard when the crowd had gone and gazed across the narrows to Kyleakin. Surely Alasdair was better now! Surely he would come soon and take this load off Jim's back! But the ferry-boat, like an active water beetle, plied back and forth and no one brought him a message even. A small, red-headed boy came to the edge of the pier and threw bits of bread to the gulls which swooped greedily to snatch them, some catching the pieces on the wing and others fishing them out of the water. The child stood laughing with pleasure. Jim took a quick look round—there was no one near. "Give me a piece!" he said. The little boy looked surprised. "It's just dry bread for the gulls," he replied. "Mummy gave it to me for the gulls." And he threw another bit over the edge.

"Give me a bit!" Jim sounded so desperate that the boy unwillingly handed over what was left. Jim snatched it from his small hand and ran behind the station buildings. Safely out of sight he chewed the crust. Seldom had anything tasted sweeter. When it was all gone he came out and watched the passenger train filling up. It looked to him like a long, red worm. People were carrying cases, buying magazines and sweets, opening purses and counting change. Amongst the crowd Jim felt very lonely with no one to talk to. His one comfort was Spot. Together they wandered back to the pens for the cattle were old friends, too. The piercing whistle of the engine as it slowly dragged the long, swaying line of carriages out of the station made him jump. He had always pictured trains as going very fast right from the start. Now he had nothing to do but wait. Had they forgotten all about him? Ought he to tell them the cattle were still waiting? He sat in a misery of indecision. Spot put his head on his knee so Jim stroked the black head and the snowy ruff round his neck and tickled him behind the ears which the dog loved.

At long last, though really it was still well short of midday,

the goods train came alongside the pens. The cattle walked into the trucks without any bother but where was he supposed to go? Seeing him hesitate the porter told him to go in the guard's van and to take the dog with him. Anyone in charge of beasts went for nothing on the train. This news was a great relief to Jim and with Spot on the rope he climbed into the guard's van at the rear of the train. There was a wooden bench along one side and after some hesitation Jim sat down on it. The guard, who was elderly and grumpy, came in. He didn't like people in his van and he particularly disliked dogs. Spot got to his feet, growling, the hair rising at the back of his head. " Keep your dog under control! " snapped the guard. Jim cuffed Spot and pushed him down but the dog went on rumbling threats deep in his throat.

" Where's the man in charge of these beasts? " demanded the guard. Jim explained timidly what had happened. The guard looked at him out of his small, red-rimmed eyes. " You're only a boy! You can't be in charge! That's breaking the regulations—it's all in the book—must be somebody in charge! Eh? What have you to say to that? There's no use just sitting there dumb! What am I to say when They ask? "

" I'm in charge," repeated Jim, not knowing what else to say, but it did nothing to soothe his questioner.

" I'm telling you, you can't be in charge! Are you deaf? Don't know what They'll say——"

Just then, with a heave and clatter, the trucks were swung into motion behind the engine. Unused to machinery of any sort Jim found the noise quite deafening. He could see by the guard's lips that he was still objecting, but he could not hear a word and it was a comfort of a sort in a world where comforts were few. At least " They " could not pounce upon him now and drag him from the train, an act of which They would be quite capable, he thought.

The railway line ran through one cutting after another and the noise, thrown back by the rocks, was very alarming. He crouched on the hard bench, shaken and downhearted, his belly rumbling. There was one small window in the front of the van and Jim would have loved to look out of it but fear of the guard kept him motionless.

The guard first read a carefully folded newspaper, then took a parcel from his satchel. Placing it firmly on his knee he unwrapped the brown paper to reveal a loaf of bread, a half-pound of butter and a lump of cheddar cheese. Holding the loaf he buttered a whole slice which he then cut off slowly and carefully with his clasp knife. Putting this down he proceeded to cut thick slices of cheese and to lay them on the bread. The boy and the dog watched every movement, each bite and the rhythmic champing of the guard's jaws, as if spellbound. A long dribble of saliva fell from Spot's mouth and Jim swallowed convulsively. The guard, for all the attention he paid his audience, might have been alone in his van. When he had finished he wrapped the remainder in brown paper, tied it with string, and put it back in the satchel which he hung on a hook beside him where it swayed slightly with the rocking of the train.

From sheer fatigue Jim fell asleep, his head falling on his chest as the train climbed the long pull up to Achnasheen. There it stood panting, waiting for the westbound train to pass. The sudden quiet awakened Jim.

"Are we there?" he cried, straightening up. No one replied; the van was empty. Jim got to his feet and almost fell because one of his legs was numb. He crossed over to the little window and saw the cattle in the truck ahead. It was a comfort for he was carrying out Alasdair's work as well as he could and surely Alasdair himself would be on the road by now! Perhaps if he had got a lift by car Jim would find him already in Dingwall. This thought gave him courage.

It was evening when the engine wheezed its way into Dingwall station. Coming out on to the busy platform after his long seclusion in the gloom of the guard's van was like coming out of a cave into daylight. The cattle trucks were drawn up beside pens.

"Putting them in?" cried a railwayman. "Aye! right, we'll give you a hand. For Baxendine's, are they?"

Jim nodded. "How can I get them a field?" he asked.

"You a stranger here? Go to Baxendine's quick, then, before the yardmen go home and they'll tell ye where to go."

" Where is Baxendine's ? "

" Out the station, across the square, take the second street on your right and you're there." The man spoke so fast in the singsong accent of Ross-shire that Jim had difficulty in understanding him. However, he had now to find the auction mart, that much was clear. If he kept his mind on the next move and on nothing but that, he found it was less frightening. He kept looking for Alasdair among the passers-by, hope rising whenever he saw farmers in tweed suits but he was not there. He took one or two wrong turnings but by dint of asking found the mart at last.

" MacAskill's cattle? Ooh! aye! we're expecting 'em. Tak' 'em through the toon tae Bowie's fairm on the hull."

" Right through the town? " Jim repeated, in his formal, school-taught English.

" Aye! Aye! " said the yardman. " There's juist the aye street tae it. Ye canna gae wrang—up the High Street and up the hull. The yett's on yer reecht-haund side. I'd send some 'un wi' ye but the loons are a' awa' tae the fitba'. Whar's the man hissel? "

Jim explained as best he could, ending by saying, " He'll be here by Monday," for the very sound of the words cheered him up. Then he hurried back to the pens, thinking that if everyone spoke like that he'd never be able to follow them. The porter was bad enough but the yardman was far worse. He discovered later that the latter was a native of Aberdeenshire and spoke the Doric.

The cattle by now were both hungry and thirsty and they bellowed as they were driven through the long, narrow High Street. There was, indeed, just the one street to the town with side streets going a short distance and ending up in fields. As the big bullocks trotted on, women swept toddlers up in their arms, small boys tagged along behind. As it was Saturday evening the place was crowded with farm folk in from the country round about to do their shopping. Motorists came to a halt waiting with what patience they could for the herd to nose past them. One sounded his horn loudly and two bullocks, thoroughly startled, broke away and made off down a side street. Jim found himself in a quandary; should he go after them and hope the rest would be all right till he got back or should he leave them? Before he had made up his mind he saw the runaways being brought back by a lanky youth.

" Going to Pringle's? " the newcomer asked.

" No, to Bowie's."

" Ah! weel, that's just straight ahead. I'll gie ye a hand."

Jim was delighted and the rest of the way up to the farm was a pleasant walk. The cattle smelt green fields and hastened their steps. Very soon they reached the gate on the right-hand side and Jim counted them as they streamed through.

Yes! they were all there, all was well; then he caught his breath—water! But even as the thought flashed through his mind he saw that the beasts had found it for themselves and were eagerly drinking out of large stone troughs, the ones behind pushing and shoving to get their share after their long, thirsty journey in the trucks. The setting sun was casting long shadows as they left the gate.

" Where are ye staying? " the lanky boy asked him.

" I don't know," Jim replied. This made the other laugh in a silly sort of way but when Jim asked him if he knew of any place he pointed up the hill to a two-storied stone cottage, saying, " There's a Mrs. Sinclair lives there. She comes from Skye and folk from the west often go to her."

This sounded grand. He could explain his penniless state to a Skye woman and he pictured her like Tom's mother or Mary Martin.

" Coming to the pictures? " the boy asked. Jim shook his head.

" Do you no' like the pictures? "

" I'm tired," Jim replied truthfully.

" Can ye gie me a bob? " was the next question.

" I haven't any money," Jim answered, blushing.

The lad's expression changed. " Meany! Meany! " he cried. "They're all mean from the west coast." He lifted his hands to his nose in a rude gesture and then slouched off downhill, shouting abuse.

Bother! thought Jim. Bother! If I'd even had a sixpence, but there was no help for it so he walked to the Sinclairs' house and knocked twice on the front door but no one came—the house was silent. He went round to the back door and knocked on it but with no result. He tried the doorhandle to see if it was locked and at that very moment a small woman carrying a heavy shopping basket, a black felt hat crammed down on her head, appeared. Putting down the basket with a thump she raised one arm, pointing to the town, and said, " Get out of that! What are you doing trying to get into my house? There's too many of your kind hanging about—work-shy! Now, clear out quick and don't try any of your tricks with me for I won't stand for them! I'll set the police on you, you and your dog. Do you hear? "

He would have been deaf, indeed, if he hadn't, for her voice was piercing. Hope fled; he knew he could explain nothing to this woman; the words died in his throat. He shuffled off forlornly, the dog at his heels. It was the last straw, he could go no farther, bear no more rebuffs. Beneath the hedge at the side of the road he flung himself down and wept like a bairn while Spot whined in sympathy.

14. The Auction Mart

He was back in school and he hadn't learnt his lessons. All the others knew their geography. "What do you call the firth which runs up to Dingwall?" the teacher was asking him. Silence. "Do you mean to say you don't know the name of the firth? I have never, no never, had a stupider pupil than you, Jim Smith." Miss Menzies gripped him by the collar and shook him several times as she had often done in the past. Well! she could shake him if she wanted to but he still didn't know the answer. He opened his eyes and looked up into the night sky, a-dazzle with stars. Confused and still in his dream he wondered why the teacher had followed him outside to hear his lesson. Cross and all as she was, she had never done that before. But someone else was talking to him now, a man.

"Look!" this person was saying, "if you can get to your feet I'll help you into the house. You can't stay here."

Could he not stay anywhere? "I wasn't doing any harm," he muttered, and was surprised how difficult it was to pronounce the words, for his lips were numb and his teeth chattering.

"No, no, it's not that," the voice said, "but it's too cold, there's a touch of frost." Yes! there must be, the stars were big as lamps in the sky. The man put an arm round his shoulders and Spot growled. The man spoke to him but the dog growled again, low and ominously.

The sound roused Jim. "Be quiet, Spot!" he ordered and struggled to get to his feet. For a few seconds, giddy with lack of food, he felt the world revolve about him and staggered·

"Steady!" said the man. "You're not well. Take my arm."

In the dark Jim did not know where they were going till he found himself once more at the door of the same house. "I can't go in here!" he protested, halting. "She chased me away."

"It's my house," replied the man and led him into the kitchen. The talk stopped abruptly when the door opened and a woman and two girls stared at the two of them.

"Archie! what are you doing—who have you got with you?"

"A boy I found outside, sleeping under the hedge. It's not the time of year for it." The man spoke mildly as if finding travellers sleeping in the cold were an everyday occurrence.

"Why! oh! dear me, it's the boy I saw this evening trying to get in!" the small woman exclaimed, putting down the sock she was knitting. Her daughters squealed and pushed back their chairs.

"Don't be silly, girls," said their father, making Jim sit down.

"You don't know who you're taking into the house, Archie," persisted his wife.

"No, I don't know who he is," replied her husband, "but I do know he's cold, hungry and homeless."

His wife was put out. She had been caught acting unkindly and she now began to justify herself. There were so many bad characters about that a body couldn't be too careful. Hadn't two hens been stolen from next door last week and their neighbour over the way had lost a can of petrol from the back of his car. Her sharp words rattled about Jim's ears like hailstones.

"Well, well, the lad wasn't here then so you can hardly blame him. You're from the west?"

"From Skye," Jim said.

"From Skye!" cried Mrs. Sinclair, stopping short in her work. "Then, why, in the name of goodness, didn't you tell me instead of standing there dumb?"

"I expect you put the fear of death on him, Annie." The man smiled.

But Mrs. Sinclair was not listening. She questioned Jim on what part of the island he came from and whether he knew so-and-so and such a one but Jim had to confess he knew very few people outside Udale. She sniffed as if to suggest that it didn't look as if he *did* come from Skye but she piled food on to his plate and never in his life had he needed food more.

"When did you eat last?" his host asked. Jim paused and looked at him, really looked at him this time. He saw a long, thin face, a large nose jutting out and not quite straight, a pair of wide, grey eyes. No one could have called him good-looking but Jim thought he had a very nice face.

"We had breakfast very early, at least it wasn't really breakfast because we were in a hurry," he said, offering it as an excuse for eating so much.

"What time was that?"

"Oh! very early, about half past four in the morning."

"And you haven't eaten anything since then?" queried Mrs. Sinclair, looking at the hands of the clock which stood at ten-thirty. Jim shook his head; he hated explaining that he had no money.

"But where were you that you couldn't get food?" she persisted, becoming more and more convinced that this was someone on the run.

"I was on the train," mumbled Jim, a picture of guilt, "with the cattle."

"Oh! you're here for the sales. Is your father with you?"

Jim shook his head. "I was with Alasdair MacAskill and he was hurt."

"Alasdair MacAskill?" she repeated, the English name

puzzling her, and then she asked, " You don't mean Alasdair Bàn, do you? "

" Yes, he was hurt this morning." Was it really only this morning? It felt half a lifetime away! Then the whole story came out and to Jim's amazement he found that Alasdair lodged in this house whenever he came to sales. Having finished his meal he sat hearing them talk without really taking in what they said. He had a curious light feeling as if he were sailing above all care or worry. Even when he heard the woman say that Alasdair must be suffering from concussion he did not really mind. All this was no more than a dream.

" Thank you, thank you," he said, for Alasdair's name reminded him of his recent lesson in manners.

" Well, it's a mercy I found you or you'd have been stiff by morning," Sinclair broke in. " Make a bed for him, wife, the lad's played out. See and give him plenty of blankets and put a hot water bottle in the bed to take the chill off the sheets."

" Do you think I don't know how to make a bed? " his wife snapped and bustled away, telling her daughters to look sharp and give her a hand. Saturday night and all this extra work!

" The dog——" Jim began uncertainly when she had gone. " Can you put him somewhere? "

" Don't you worry about the dog," replied Archie. " I'll see he gets a place in the scullery and a bowl of food. He's hungry, too, eh? Now, you take a long lie in the morning, I'll take a wee keek at the beasts myself, so you've nothing to worry about."

Jim grinned weakly with relief. Here was a friend, indeed. He followed Mrs. Sinclair to the room which struck damp and cold but the bed was warm and almost at the moment his head touched the pillow he was sound asleep.

Back in the kitchen Mrs. Sinclair fired off one last volley in defence of her actions. " Of all the gormless creatures! " she declared as she tidied up for the night. " Not to have the wit to borrow money from the auctioneers and him with all those beasts to sell on Monday! Worth hundreds of pounds, I suppose. I've never yet come across anyone so green!"

"I wouldn't say that!" argued her husband—he was fond of arguing. "He took the cattle here all by himself and for a laddie out of a far-off island I think he did pretty well considering." But his wife, lowering the wick of the lamp, felt she would never really forgive the boy for her own mistake.

Sunday passed calm as a pool in a river when the water's low. It was noon before Sinclair woke Jim, telling him he could have a wash in the scullery before Mrs. Sinclair and the daughters came home from the kirk. Jim washed himself to such good purpose that his hair was standing on end and his ears were as red as the sun seen through fog. Archie offered him the use of his comb so at dinner he was a very different looking boy from the vagabond of the night before. The sight of the young ladies in their Sunday finery, however, deprived him of all speech save "thank you" to which he clung; so much so that the girls were in danger of going off into a fit of giggles if he said it only once more.

But out in the field with the cattle and Spot that afternoon Jim was quite happy. He looked down on the little town, watching the smoke rising from all the chimneys into the still autumn air and thought what a lot of people there were in the world. The size of the fields astonished him. Why, the Bruces could have put their whole croft into that one field easy and room left over. Towards evening the church bells began to ring " ding-dong, ding-dong." One belfry after another joined in making this melancholy noise till the whole valley was a clamour of bells. Just then Jim saw Archie Sinclair coming through the gate.

"Come into your tea," he said, "they're off to the kirk. Oh! bring Spot in with you. We'll put him out to the shed before they come back."

Jim was delighted to know that they had the house to themselves. He was not shy with Archie and talked freely to him about Alasdair and the cattle and of how they had herded them for a whole year keeping them from the trees. The man listened with great interest.

" Well! to think of that! So they were getting the good of the grass and not harming the young trees! That was a good plan. It is just a pity that prices have fallen so low. We're in a slump, that's what they call it, a slump. It means there's no price for anything. Slumps and booms, slumps and booms," he murmured, more to himself than to Jim, " and, yet, can you explain this? Why is a beast worth, say, thirty pounds one year and the next he's worth only ten? If he's the same weight he'll feed as many people so why the drop?"

This was more than Jim could answer. He'd never even heard a question like that before. Alasdair had told him plenty about prices rising and falling but he had taken such things for granted. Prices always did rise and fall and that was that. Archie laughed when he saw Jim's puzzled look. " That's a poser, isn't it? I don't think many people do know the answer. I'm a cobbler and when I'm mending boots and shoes I have time to puzzle my head over questions like these and I puzzle my customers, too!"

Jim was up early next morning. He and Spot understood each other by now and drove the cattle through the town despite all the hazards of milk and dust carts. Outside Baxendine's he stood for a moment recalling exactly how Alasdair had wanted the cattle penned. A yardman came and began to push the wrong ones together.

" Not that way!" Jim cried.

" What way, then? We haven't all day to be staring about us. There'll be more cattle in to-day than we can well handle."

Jim did not dispute this but it was not his affair. *His* beasts must be penned correctly, come what may. He drove out the wrong bullocks, found the other pair which matched, drove them into the pen, and closed the gate on his first lot.

"It's lucky ye came early!" mocked the man. "If ye was to take all that time an hour hence ye'd hold the whole sale up!"

Jim reddened through his tan. He knew he was doing this slowly and he could imagine how quickly Alasdair would do it but the man was no help. You mustn't, whatever you did, put a poorer beast in alongside better ones or you'd spoil your price for the good ones. He hadn't been a year with Alasdair without grasping that.

At last he had them all penned just right and could afford to take it easy and look about him. The yard was seething with cattle, drovers, dogs, and yardmen, and the noise was overpowering. The Aberdonian whom he had seen on Saturday noticed him just then and had time for a friendly word. "Got 'em all in? Good! Did ye fin' yer place in the catalogue?"

Jim looked puzzled. "Ye hanna got yer catalogue? Weel, awa' to the office, they'll gie ye ane. That way ye ken when yer own lots are coming in. The office is just roon there, first door on yer recht."

Jim found the office and then stood hesitating; if he knocked and they came what could he say? Suppose he had to pay? He might have stood a long time in that musty, dusty passage if the door had not been thrown open suddenly by a big, burly man in a plus-four suit.

"Who's there?" he cried, sensing rather than seeing the boy in the dim light.

"I was wanting a catalogue," Jim said.

"What? What? Speak up, man."

"A catalogue!" Jim repeated.

"Oh! aye, well, there's no need to shout. Gi'e him a catalogue, Davie, man." The person so addressed was a tall, incredibly thin youth with a bird-like head on his lean shoulders.

" What's the like o' you wanting a catalogue for?" this individual asked him.

" To find—well, to find when my beasts come in."

The youth guffawed. " Your faither's beasts, ye mean." He handed over two catalogues. " There's one for yourself and one for your dad."

Jim didn't wait to argue. For the first time it struck him that they might ask whether he had the right to sell the cattle. But they had to be sold, hadn't they? Suddenly his knees felt weak and a taste of sickness came into his mouth. Afraid of vomiting, he pushed past people into the open and leant against the side of a monument in the Square till the cool morning air made him feel better. This was no time for panic, he chided himself. But suppose prices were very bad, would he have to take them home? The very thought scared him. " I can't do it alone! I can't, I can't do it alone! Oh! why doesn't Alasdair come or send word? A new and horrible idea came into his head—perhaps Alasdair had died! Panic came surging back but he had the sense to resist. As it happened a herd of cross-highland cattle was just passing and he forced himself to study them and guess what price they would make in the ring. Some of them, he admitted grudgingly, were nearly as good as any off Brae. Would they reach twelve pounds or stop at eleven? He puzzled over it and then found to his great relief that the feeling of sickness had passed. I'll keep my mind on the cattle, he thought, and that'll keep me from worrying. He went in and took a place at the ringside. Farmers were coming in by twos and threes, joking and chaffing each other. Nobody seemed to have a care in the world except himself.

The auctioneer was in his box and the first cattle were coming into the ring. They were good beasts but they did not make ten pounds. Jim's heart somersaulted downwards. The big farmer beside him leant his chin on the clasped hands holding his tall crook. " Huh!" was his only comment. Jim took a look at the catalogue, running his finger down the list till he came to

" Cross-Highland bullocks—Brae." That was his first lot and the last one came near the end of the sale.

" Bad to be first in the catalogue," remarked a small man in a shabby raincoat on his right.

" What's the best place? " asked Jim.

" About the middle on an ordinary day but near the end if there's a rise."

" Then if there's a fall you'd be better near the beginning? "

" Well, it's this way, boy, if prices fall much lower we'll be giving them away—making presents of them, like."

The next lot did a little better but they deserved to. By the time Jim's turn was coming near they were making ten pounds.

" I'd better go and fetch them," Jim said to his neighbour.

" Na! Na! The yairdmen 'ull put 'em in the ring for ye. A' ye hae tae dae is pit 'em roon the ring. New tae these pairts? Aye, weel, just wait here. An' if ye don't want to sell say, ' No!' loud and clear so's there'll be nae mistake. Mind ye, the bottom's oot o' the mairket, might as well sell up and let the wife take lodgers." And here the little man laughed heartily as if it was the best joke in the world, but Jim was too strung up to heed him. His bullocks came into the ring at that moment, real beauties, carrying themselves proudly the way beasts do which have been suckled by their mothers as calves. There was a stir of interest in the crowd. " Fine, hardy bullocks," the auctioneer was saying. " Move them around, boy, till everyone has a look. Real toppers—now, gen'l'm'n, what am I bid? Who'll give me a start? Ten pounds? Come along, gen'l'm'n, you won't see better the day. Nine pounds, then? Eight pounds? You'll be sorry you missed them—seven pounds, I'm bid, and ten—thank you—and fifteen—eight pounds, eight pounds I'm bid, grand two-year-olds, and five—and ten, thank you, sir——" The bidding went fast and yet to Jim's inexperienced eye no one made a sign but still the price went up, now by ten shillings, now by a mere half crown. He was so bewildered by the speed that the auctioneer was saying, "Ten pounds, going at ten pounds, going at ten pounds——" He had just time to gasp out "No!" before the hammer came down.

"Well, we'll have another try——" and this time his efforts drove the price to ten guineas but there it stuck. "Going at ten guineas——"

"No!"

"Come along, young man, you're getting a fair crack of the whip, we're not getting the prices we used to after the war—when you were in your cradle——" There was a general laugh but not another shilling could the auctioneer get.

"Take them out, I can't do better for you." The yardmen drove the bullocks out, a fresh lot came in. Flushed and downhearted, Jim went back to his place. It had been filled in his absence but by dint of using his elbows the little man let him in. To Jim's surprise he did not blame him. "Na! Na! Ye did fine. Best bullocks to-day. Should have made twelve pounds—far better than the lot from Scourie and they made eleven. Try 'em again at the end, lad."

The big farmer said something like "Hurrumph!" Much encouraged, Jim watched each lot as it went through and carefully noted the prices. The small man was right (and so, of course, was Alasdair). According to the prices being made his should have reached twelve pounds. Then his heifers came in. They were bonny, too, of a yellow-brown colour with a touch of white on their bellies. This time everything went swimmingly. Eleven pounds was Alasdair's price and they reached it. "Going—going—gone." This time Jim nodded.

"Grand!" commented his friend. "Mind ye, ye might, just *might* have screwed another five shillings out o' them but ye got a guid price."

"It was eleven pounds Alasdair said."

"Well! he wasnae far oot. Where is he, the day?"

Jim told him what had happened. The little man listened
intently.

"So you're in charge? Well, he's no doing sae bad, your
Alasdair."

The little man then took him away for a cup of tea and a
mutton pie. If left to himself Jim would have stayed all day at
the ringside for the excitement of the bidding had got hold of him,
but when his friend put a pie into his hand he ate it and found it
good.

Late in the afternoon the last pen of bullocks was driven in. They were not so good as the first pen and Alasdair had priced them at ten pounds. They made ten guineas. Jim was delighted, scarcely crediting his luck. But he had still his six best bullocks on his hands. He'd have to try them now.

Suddenly the big farmer who hadn't said a word all day barked out, " What's your price for the bullocks ? "

If a post had spoken Jim could not have been more astonished.

" T-t-twelve pounds," he managed to stammer.

" Done ! " They shook hands on it and before Jim's goggling eyes the farmer produced fourteen five-pound notes, one pound note, and two ten-shilling notes. " What name ? "

" Alasdair MacAskill, Brae."

" Well, ye can gi'e me a luckpenny."

Jim hesitated, not knowing what to give. " Give him the two pounds," whispered the wee man. Jim handed them over and the big man nodded his thanks.

" I'll take possession," he said. All three left the ringside and threaded a way through the crowd to the pens which were now empty except for the bullocks.

" Where are they going to ? " the wee man asked, saying aside to Jim, " Your Alasdair will want to know."

" Cloothie, Inverurie," replied the other, as saving of words as ever.

So Jim watched the bullocks he had herded so often in the past year heading away for the railway station. They went at a half-trot, bellowing one to the other, hoping for green fields.

The sale on the Tuesday followed much the same pattern. His first pen made what Alasdair had hoped for, the next did slightly better but the third lot fell a pound short and Jim refused to sell. He looked about for the little man who had been so helpful but neither he nor the big farmer were present. Would anyone come to his rescue this time ? At any rate, there was still time. Just then someone tapped him on the shoulder.

" You're wanted in the office."

" In the office? But I'm selling—I can't come."

" You'll have to come; it's the boss that's wanting you," the message-boy persisted.

Surprised and puzzled, Jim squeezed his way out of the ring, the familiar cries of the auctioneer—" Eleven pounds I'm bid, come along, gen'l'm'n, and five and ten, thank *you*, this very fine lot—" growing fainter as he made his way along the narrow passage to the office. This time the youth who had fetched him opened it. Davie, the tall, thin chap who sat facing it, looked up from his ledger and said, " Here's the culprit! "

An elderly, grey-haired man with a large, florid face, swung round from the fire to look at him. The silence could be felt.

" Well! " he said at last in a choked wheeze of a voice. " So you're Jim Smith, eh? "

The boy nodded, and the man broke out, " What do you mean by it, eh? You've landed us in a rare spot of bother, you have! Now, what have you got to say for yourself? "

Jim didn't know where to begin and stood gaping. The big man coughed and wheezed some more, reminding Jim of the goods engine getting up a head of steam, and then he burst out angrily, " Well! come on, say something! Here we've been selling cattle without the owner's consent! Now, explain what you mean by it. Were you going to make a bolt with the money? Was that your game? "

" No," Jim said. " I'm not going off with any money. I'm selling the cattle for Alasdair MacAskill."

" Did Mr. MacAskill tell you to sell them? You tell the truth, now, or it'll be the worse for you."

The man's red face and beaked nose hung over Jim so close that he could have counted the hairs in his wide nostrils.

" No, but——"

His interrogator made an explosive sound. " What good is that to us? You've made us party to a fraud, neither more nor less. Here we've got to find the buyers and tell them the cattle weren't ours to sell and some of them will have reached Stirling by now. Now do you see what you have done?" With an abrupt movement the man turned his back on Jim. "Saunders!" he said. "Tell MacBeth to come here. Put someone else into the box till we get to the bottom of this."

Saunders went out at once. Jim was left standing miserably in the middle of the office, scraping his feet on the shabby, worn linoleum. He had been afraid the day before that something like this would happen and then he had forgotten all about it in the excitement of the sales. What a pity they hadn't let him finish! He'd lose his place in the catalogue if they didn't hurry up and then what would he do? The sickly green walls hemmed him in; he read and re-read the advertisements on the calendar hanging on the wall until at last Saunders appeared with the auctioneer at his heels.

"What's up?" asked MacBeth.

"This!" The elderly man handed him a telegram which Macbeth read aloud. "Keep cattle till next week. MacAskill." He looked up, puzzled. "Who's MacAskill?"

"You know him—Alasdair Bàn," said Saunders, picking his teeth—he was thoroughly enjoying this spot of bother. "Used to do a bit of dealing and now he's got the Brae grazings."

"Oh! Brae—well, if you'd said that at first I'd have known what you were talking about—very nice beasts, too. I got a good price for them, Mr. Henderson, both for the highlanders and crosses yesterday, and for the polls to-day."

"You got all you could for them?" asked Mr. Henderson, stretching across the desk for the telegram.

"Of course I did; I'm telling you they were good beasts, some were going at twelve pounds, some at eleven pounds, ten— oh! I got every penny I could screw out of them, not a doubt about that, except, wait a minute, let me see, yes, there was one pen didn't reach the price the boy wanted, well, he didn't sell."

" Where are they, then ? " The gimlet grey eyes bored into Jim who replied falteringly:

" I sold them at the end of the sale."

" Get a good price for them ? "

" Twelve pounds—that's what Alasdair wanted. I wouldn't sell till I got the price but I did get it."

Mr. Henderson rubbed his cheek upward with his hand, making a rasping sound against the bristle. He was taken aback as he afterwards admitted; it was a state unusual for him.

" Well! I'm jiggered. Look, wire Mr. MacAskill, Davie, tell him the beasts sold at a good price. Ask him if it's O.K. Tell him he won't get as good a price next week for it's only a small sale beside this one."

As Davie scribbled this down Mr. Henderson turned like a prosecuting lawyer on to Jim once more.

" How did you know what price Mr. MacAskill wanted? Who told you ? "

Jim explained haltingly in his careful English how he had come to be in charge.

" Is he better ? " he found courage to ask at the end of his recital.

" If he's started worrying about cattle he must be," was the dry response. " Where's he wiring from, Davie? Broadford? If he's still in the hospital he must have got himself some crack."

" I'd better be getting back," said the auctioneer.

" Wait a minute, man, till we get this straight. You stand by that, do you, George, he couldn't have got a better price if he'd been here himself ? "

" That's right, Mr. Henderson, it's the truth. I'd swear to it in court."

" Can I go now ? " Jim asked, his anxiety overcoming his shyness. " There's the last lot——"

" You'll not sell another hoof till we get this cleared up. Get that wire off, Davie, it'll go through to-night, yet. How many's left?" This last remark was shot in Jim's direction.

"One lot of poll bullocks still to come in and a pen of heifers that didn't reach the price in the morning."

Henderson nodded, drumming his thick fingers on the desk for a minute before breaking out angrily, "You should have told us! Man alive! Thousands of cattle going through our hands, the biggest sale of the autumn—how were we to ken? Can we be expected to keep track of every bare-faced loon?"

Saunders went out and Henderson slumped down behind the desk. He pulled a crushed packet of fags out of a pocket and lit one.

"Well, the best thing you can do is to get back to that God-forsaken island of yours and see MacAskill. Maybe he'll eat you alive, maybe he won't, that's his affair. Catch the evening train. If he's agreeable to the sale we'll send him on his cheque."

But Jim still hesitated. "Could I not just sell the last of them?"

The big man exploded. "No! Get out! That's enough. If you stay here just one more minute I'll set the police on you——" Before he could finish his tirade Jim had fled. Henderson broke into a rumbling belly laugh. That made him shift, he thought. I hope MacAskill won't turn nasty. I don't believe he will. He knows the market.

Jim made his way into the open air. Sunshine was flooding the little town, children were playing in the streets. He paused, uncertain what to do next. Now that the strain of selling was over he felt limp and so tired he could hardly put one foot in front of the other. He thought of his friend the shoemaker and made his way to his shop. It was no more than a little dark room at the bottom of a side street. Sinclair was running a machine and didn't hear the door open. Jim gazed in surprise at all the shoes filling every shelf and overflowing on to the rough wooden counter. The shoemaker stopped the machine and turned round.

" Oh! it's you, Jim, I didn't hear you come in—how did it go to-day, lad ? "

Jim poured out his story, a mixture of triumph and defeat. Archie listened to every word with his whole attention. When Jim came to an end he shook his head saying, " Well! Well! that was a pity, a pity he had to send that wire and you doing so well. Anyway, you know you did the best you could and no one can do more than that. Come, have you had a square meal to-day ? I guessed as much. Well, I'm my own master. We'll just shut up shop and they must wait another wee while for their shoes."

" I've to catch the train," said Jim, nervously.

" Well, we have an hour till then, plenty of time." So saying, Archie took off his apron, put on a cap, and off they went together up to the High Street.

" What about buying yourself something ? " said Archie, noticing Jim's eyes straying to the shop windows. They were outside a bicycle shop and that reminded Jim of Tom's old bicycle—well, it was his father's really, the pump was terrible. When you were pumping a flat tyre it took ages because air hissed out at every stroke.

" Could I get a bicycle pump ? "

" And why not ? " retorted Archie and took him straight into the shop. The gleaming bicycles, tricycles, prams, and go-carts reduced Jim to an awed silence so Archie carried out the transaction for him except that when it came to paying Jim took out his wad of notes. " Perhaps I shouldn't use these," he whispered. " They're no' mine."

" Nonsense ! " said the shoemaker decisively. " You haven't asked for much and you've earned a wage. You'd better give me a pound for the wife and if she wants more she can get it from Alasdair next week if he's fit to sell the rest then."

His words made Jim realise fully that Alasdair was going to recover, he wasn't going to be in hospital for weeks and weeks far less die. He felt quite light-headed from a mixture of relief and hunger. From the shop they went to the station restaurant where the shoemaker ordered soup to be followed by mutton stew. Jim sat back, thankful to be looked after. With the bicycle pump beside him he made a hearty meal and was pleased when Archie coaxed the waitress into giving Spot some scraps.

It was blue dusk when they came out on the platform. Archie bought Jim's ticket and waited beside him till the engine came thundering towards them, alarming Jim and terrifying Spot out of his wits. He would have run away except for Jim's grip of him. Archie found them a seat, gave Jim a bundle of comics, and was there waving good-bye when the train moved out.

Jim sat with the comics unopened on his knee as the engine climbed and climbed and then plunged through the " cut," its wheels going round to the words, " I am so happy," " I am so happy." It was one of life's great moments. He had carried out his task in face of difficulties and now he was on his way to tell the whole story to Alasdair.

15. *Homeward Bound*

It was a very dark night and Jim felt rather than saw his way
through the avenue of trees to the hospital. It stood facing the
bay and a light shining from the front door drew Jim to the
porch where he pressed his nose against the glass-panelled inner
door. There was no one to be seen in the small front hall, not a
sound to be heard. The little hospital was bathed in calm. Jim
stood there for some time hoping to see someone. At last, out
of patience, he turned the handle very gently, but as bad luck
would have it at that very moment a beautiful black cat, proud
as Lucifer, came stepping daintily across the parquet floor. Spot,
who could not abide cats, and had had his nose to the crack,
·flung himself, slithering wildly on the polished floor, straight at
the brute. At the same moment the ward door opened, a little
nurse stepped out carrying a tray, and the cat sprang clawing its
way up her starched apron. The nurse screamed, dropping the
tray with a loud crash, the cat spat, the dog barked, and patients'
heads popped out from all quarters.

"Spot!" cried Jim, and "Spot!" shouted a deeper voice.
Jim looked up and there was Alasdair in blue and white striped
pyjamas, a bandage on his head. Together they seized the dog,
another patient grabbed the terrified cat and was well scratched
for his pains, the nurse clasped her neck, and women patients in
long dressing gowns came fussing round her.

"Jim!" cried Alasdair, and "Oh! Alasdair——" cried Jim,
but that was all they had time for. The little nurse, her eyes
flashing furiously, came between them.

" I might have known it! " she declared. " Another of your dogs, Mr. MacAskill! Isn't it enough that I have to be stepping over your dog no matter where I go but now this boy comes along with a worse one? "

" Oh! nurse—— " began Alasdair, in his most wheedling tone, but she would have none of it.

" Don't you ' Oh! nurse ' me, Alasdair Bàn! These scratches will go septic, I know they will, and that will be your doing, you and your horrible dogs! "

At this, all the females with their hair in curl papers groaned and murmured, " That's what will happen, oh! yes, to be sure," though Jim was certain they had no more idea what septic meant than he had.

" Out of here! " The nurse bore down on Jim like a small but deadly destroyer. He backed away, clutching the still excited Spot by the neck.

" Oh! nurse, just a minute, only a minute, he's my man of business, he's got news for me—— "

But she would not listen. " Out of this hospital and don't show your face here again! "

Jim, still hoping that Alasdair would cope, looked round and saw that, far from coping, he had gone. He was done for now and no mistake! Outside he cuffed the wretched Spot, cause of all these goings on. Just then the window beside him was thrown up and Alasdair's head appeared.

" Did you sell them, Jim? "

" Yes, yes—— "

" What did the big roan bullocks make? "

" Twelve pounds."

" Good lad! And the cross-highland heifers?—Oh! good life, she's coming! Go to my cousin's again to-night and come here to the window in the morning! " Alasdair's head was suddenly withdrawn, the window came down with a bang, waking the only patient who had slept through the preceding riot.

In the morning Jim came back, this time without Spot who had been locked in a shed and was even then howling his heart out. It was a lovely autumn morning, sunshine playing on every little wave in the bay and the mainland hills gently etched in blue.

Jim had only the gravel drive between him and Alasdair's window but he stood hesitating. They'd hear him crossing it. Should he sit down and take his boots off? But before he could decide the door opened and the nurse came out.

" You again! " she said. " I thought I told you last night not to show your face here again? "

Jim hadn't a word to say. Suddenly she laughed, showing very white teeth.

"Oh! come in, he's eating his heart out and lucky for you the poisoning hasn't set in yet. Here's your visitor!" she announced to Alasdair, showing Jim into the small ward. " Perhaps we'll have some peace now! Get into your bed, for goodness' sake, you'll give yourself a relapse and if Matron finds out what's been going on there'll be wigs on the green! Sit down, boy, and no nonsense till I come back."

So saying, the little nurse adjusted a bedcover or two and whisked away, but no sooner had the door closed behind her than all the patients, except the very old man in the corner, popped their heads up and listened to every word of Jim's saga with " Ohs!" and "Ahs!" of sympathy, " Well! Wells! " expressing admiration when he was getting good prices to " Och! Ochs! " of sympathy when he was led off to Mr. Henderson's office.

"Willie Henderson!" exclaimed Alasdair. " Oh! Willie's an old friend of mine—oh! he was doing it for the best, aye! he's straight, is Willie, and the kind of man you'd sooner have on your side than against you. Oh! well, if only I'd stayed quiet! But how was I to know what was happening! You should have sent a wire, Jim."

Such an idea had never crossed Jim's mind.

" I didn't know how you were!" he protested. " Mrs. Sinclair said you'd be weeks, you might even die!"

The patient in the next bed remarked it would take more than a knock on the head to send Alasdair to the next world, especially at sale time.

Alasdair banged the palm of his hand with his closed fist.

" How many are left? And they say it'll be a poor sale next week? Well, wasn't I the donkey? I might have known you wouldn't let me down, Jim."

These words were sweet in Jim's ears. He flushed with pleasure and just then the nurse came in with tea and digestive biscuits.

" You're not to excite yourselves," she said repressively. " The matron and the doctor will be coming round quite soon. Have a cup of tea, Jim, but then you must go. She wasn't half mad this morning when she saw all those broken cups! I'll be looking for my share of all those thousands you've been making!"

" And you'll get that, nurse, for a better nurse a man couldn't hope to have. It's almost worth a crack on the head just to come here——"

" Aren't you the one! It's easy to see you make your living by your tongue! It's well oiled."

Jim had just time to drink a cup of tea when she came back to tell him he must go. Alasdair shook him warmly by the hand, saying, " You and me will have to wean the calves when I get back from the sales. You've been a grand help, lad."

The last glimpse Jim had of him was sitting up in bed scribbling figures on the margin of the newspaper, his brow furrowed with the effort.

Jim dropped off the bus that afternoon with a five-mile walk ahead of him. Spot, glad to be clear of vehicles, dashed down the road, giving short, ecstatic barks of pleasure. This smells like home, he seemed to be saying, as he came racing back only to dash off once more.

" Take it easy, man!" Jim rebuked him but he, too, was glad

184

to be nearing the end of his journey. The sunshine of the fore-
noon had given way to a drizzle of light rain. Jim put on Tom's
coat and arranged his parcels comfortably. He had bought in
the Broadford store a grand new walking stick for Donald, a
pipe for Finlay, and a box of chocolates for Sarah. He had
hesitated a long time over this last purchase not feeling sure what
she would like. Now he put the box of chocolates and the pipe
in one pocket, the pump in the other and, holding Donald's
stick in his hand, he set out at an easy pace.

It was exactly a week since the day he and Alasdair had set
out together on their long trek which was to have so unexpected
a climax. Good thing I didn't know, he reflected, if I'd seen myself
having to go on alone I'd have turned tail and run home but
when I had to do it, I managed. I know I did a lot of silly things
but that doesn't matter, I'd know better another time. It's silly
to be afraid of things, he thought, quickening his pace a little,
I'm not going to be afraid of things any longer, I'll speak up,
say what I think and not tell lies or do things on the sly. I'll
work for them since they brought me up but I'll work along
with Alasdair, too; there's plenty of time to do both. When
I'm a little older I'll get a full-time job on a farm and work till I
get money for a place of my own. For a while he was lost in
daydreams, seeing himself taking his own cattle into the ring,
hearing the murmurs all round, " Smith's cattle? Good beasts
—you could do worse than buy Smith's." By the time he had
reached the distillery peat stack he had a farm stocked with a
pedigree highland herd.

From there the road ran downhill to his own home. He
thought of Tom. He'd go round to see him that very evening as
soon as he had a meal. He had his coat to give back and then
what fun he'd have telling Tom about everything that had
happened. The evening would hardly be long enough. But now
amongst familiar hills he was brought up against the thought of
his own home. What sort of welcome awaited him there? He

should have been back last Friday and it was now Wednesday. He tried to shrug it off; it had been no fault of his nor wish of his either for that matter. But a chill, cold feeling remained and a cloud came over his mood just as cloud had darkened the morning sunshine.

The smell of the place! Sarah had the habit of throwing dirty water out at the back door—not only water but potato peelings, tea leaves, fish bones, and the dregs of the soup. This liquid lay greasily between the cobblestones and smelt sour. Gosh! the place could do with a clean up! He compared it to the neat farm-steads of Easter Ross. If Alasdair's cattle left him time he'd get at it with a broom next day.

No one was about. In spite of his resolutions he opened the door furtively, creeping into the scullery, the stale smell of it striking him afresh. All was quiet but it was a listening quiet as if there were people lying in wait for him. Quite suddenly he felt fear coming over him, blind fear. He must get away, get away quick before they could catch him. This was the house where he had been miserable all his life. Nothing had changed. He groped for the doorhandle but at the same instant a hand caught him by the collar and swung him round. Sarah confronted him.

"So you made off!" she said, shaking him backwards and forwards. "So you did just as you pleased! What did you care for the people who brought you up and fed and clothed you? Nothing, just nothing. You left them for a rascally drover, no kith or kin of yours, but a man with soft ways to him and a flattering tongue! If I hadn't taken you out of a slum you'd have starved, do you hear? Starved! And your miserable, cheating, pinched face wouldn't be here now in front of me. And that's what you get and *that* and *that*!"

With each word she slapped his face first on one side and then on the other till his ears rang. When she let go of him he staggered and caught the edge of the table to steady himself.

"Don't!" he pleaded. "Don't! It wasn't my fault—I couldn't help it—I had to go—Alasdair was hurt——"

But she did not listen to a word of explanation. She was deaf, imprisoned in her own anger. She stormed on, telling him what a burden he had been, how they had had to pinch and scrape to keep food to his mouth. Everything he had ever done wrong from breaking dishes when he was small, kicking through the toes of his boots, letting the cows into the corn, upsetting the cream jar to breaking the big lamp on his last day at school came

out in one wild spate of abuse. The boy was overwhelmed, his new-found manliness draining away faster than water out of a sink when the stopper is removed. Suddenly her tone changed. She was looking at the parcels sticking out of his pockets and then her eye travelled to the stick lying on the floor.

"Brought us home a stick to beat you with?" she said, sarcastically, as she waved it above his head. He cringed.

"You're a wee coward," she went on, quite conversationally. "I'd have liked you better if you'd had a bit more spirit but you're just a wee coward. I bet when you were walking down the road you were saying to yourself how brave you were going to be, eh?" She laughed when she saw that her taunt went home. "But you can't, you know, you can't stand up to me, you never could."

She took the parcels from his pocket. "What's this? A pipe for Finlay? Doesn't he smoke enough already, the dirty old——" She flung the pipe down so that it broke. "And this? What's this?' She fingered the paper round the box of chocolates.

"I bought you—a—a present."

"A present? You bought me a present? Well! I'll show you what I think of your present, you bad, bad, disobedient boy." By this time she was tearing the paper off the box, her voice rising and falling in a kind of chant. She gazed a minute at the roses, then snatched the lid off and let the whole contents scatter over the dirty cement floor, so that fancy papers glittered from dark corners and white cream oozed from broken chocolate. "That's what I think of your present, see? It's not presents I want but you doing what you're told and that's what you'll do from now on." She had calmed down once more and in an ordinary tone said, "Go to your room. You will work here with your father and your uncle. There'll be no more running away up to Brae. You'll stay here and do what you're told. Go on! Go to your room!"

Like a sleep-walker he moved towards the kitchen door in the grip of the habit of a lifetime. He had always had to obey

Sarah. He felt the bicycle pump still in his pocket. *That* he still had and his hand tightened over it as if to save it. At once she noticed the gesture. If she had been content with her victory he would have gone to his room but after months of restraint her anger had spilt over and she was carried away helplessly on its flood. She could not leave him alone. Seeing his hand on the parcel she grabbed it, dragged off the brown paper and the beautiful silver and blue pump glinted in the twilight.

"Leave my pump alone!" Jim cried.

She glared at him but this time he defied her. "It's Tom's pump and you leave it alone. *I* bought it."

She gave a wild laugh as if enjoying the renewed struggle. "It's Tom's pump, is it? I'll show you, my young cockerel, whose pump it is." And she looked about for some way of destroying it. It was now or never if he was to save it. He sprang but she shook him off, dragged an iron pot from under the table, and brought the pump down on the rim with all her might. The blue enamel cracked and flaked off in a spray of tiny particles. Jim had succeeded in getting a grip of it and now tried to wrest it from her but she was too strong for him.

"You think you're strong!" she mocked him. "And you can't take a pump from me!" To tease him further she made as to let go, then pulled it back. Seeing his weakness she laughed and let him pull her farther but she had forgotten the iron pot. Jim gave an extra hard pull, the pot caught her, she tripped and fell, striking her nose on the edge of the table. At once blood came pouring out. She began to make weird noises, like an animal choking. In the struggle her long, black hair had come loose and with this and the blood streaming over her mouth and chin she looked hardly human. Scared out of his wits Jim groped for the door knob. She was dazed for the moment but as soon as she came to she'd do him in. That was for sure. He got outside somehow and began to run. The October twilight swallowed him up.

16. Outlawed

"Is Jim not home, yet, Tom?" his mother asked him as she poured out tea for the whole family.

"No," said Tom. "But I expect he'll be home to-night, or maybe to-morrow if the sale went on too long."

"Fancy Jim having to go alone! I do hope Alasdair's better." They had heard on Monday from the postman what had happened.

At that very moment the door was flung open without ceremony and the two Bruces came into the kitchen. Taken by surprise the whole family gazed at them speechless.

"Give me the boy, Murdo!" Donald said. He had a wild light in his eye and mistaking their silence for guilt he repeated even more threateningly, "Give me the boy!"

Murdo rose to his feet. "Is it Jim you mean? He's not here, Donald——"

"You're hiding him! You're hiding him! But do you know what he is? A murderer!"

Effie shrieked and the young children set up a wail. Tom looked at his father and was comforted to see him calm.

"That's no way to talk!" he rejoined. "Come, Donald, sit down, man, and tell us what's wrong and we'll help you."

Their neighbour, William Ross, who was sitting by the fire, remarked afterwards to his wife that it had been as good as a play.

"I will not sit down!" Donald shouted. "Did I not find

her in a pool of blood? Ask *him* where he is." He waved his
stick at Tom.

"Look, Donald, Jim's been in Dingwall this last week. How
could Tom see him?"

"He's not in Dingwall now! We've seen his handiwork and
we're going to find him. This is where he was last time and I'm
going to search every nook and cranny."

Murdo looked at his son. Tom shook his head but they
could not persuade the Bruces that they were telling the truth.
At last Murdo unhooked the lantern and the little band went out
to the barn. Owing to the good harvest it was packed right up
to the top. It was all Tom could do to squeeze a way in and
quite impossible for a grown man to follow him but this only
served to convince Donald that Jim lay between the roof and
the hay in some scooped out hollow. Tom had to pull out
great wads of grass to show them there was nothing behind but
more and more of it, tightly stemmed. Foiled there, they
insisted on searching the byre and the stable. The lantern threw
enormous shadows and brought Tom's heart to his mouth, sure
that he had caught a glimpse of Jim lurking just beyond the pool
of light. If they find him, he thought, they'll kill him. They
poked into barrels, searched behind harness, ransacked the cart-
shed. But it was worse when they stood still and listened. Was
that breathing he heard? No, it was nothing; the cry of a bird
out at sea broke the stillness, an owl hooted from the graveyard.

"He's here somewhere!" Donald cried, with all the
obstinacy of a weak man. Murdo pushed back his cap and
wiped his face which was streaming with sweat.

"If he's here, we'll find him. Come into the house and
rest. You're all done in."

"I must go back! I must go back! The wife's hurt." But
he let Murdo draw him into the house. William Ross made off
home with the news, for such excitements did not occur every
day.

Murdo gave each of them a dram. " Is Sarah bad, Donald ? " Effie asked timidly, afraid to provoke a fresh outburst but anxious to know.

" Didn't I find her in a pool of blood ? " he repeated wildly, " and what must I do now ? "

" You'll need to get the doctor——"

Donald put his empty glass down on the table. " She will not hear of the doctor—Kursty Morag is with her."

" Oh! If Kursty Morag is with her she has the best nurse in the place," said Effie, thankful that she herself could stay at home. The Bruces had always frightened her.

" Aye! Aye! the best nurse," echoed Finlay, who had swallowed his whisky in one gulp and was now regretfully eyeing the empty bottle.

" I'll walk back with you," said Murdo, and the three men went out.

" Well, I never ! " exclaimed Effie, falling into a seat. " There's your father off without his tea and what can have come over Jim to do a thing like that ? "

" He'd do anything," said Mary.

" He nearly did for me," chimed in Donnie, who was at home for the long week-end.

" He never did! " retorted Tom angrily. " You and him had fights, that was all! He never hurt Sarah, Mother, I know he didn't, it's something *she's* done. She was always at him, you know she was! "

" Oh! Tom, they brought him up and he wasn't their own——"

" Yes, and they always let him know it, didn't they ? "

" If he hadn't done something wrong he wouldn't have run away," said Donnie, proud of his logic but unprepared for its effect on Tom.

" If you say another word against him I'll knock you down! "

" Tom! Your own brother! " cried his mother, scandalised,

but Donnie, looking at Tom, saw that he meant exactly what he said. He held his tongue.

The news flew round the township. "Well, isn't that awful!" cried William's wife. "You hear of that kind of thing happening in Glasgow. Of course, that's just where he came from, after all. You never know with children you bring home."

In the Macdonalds' Alec John recounted with glee the terrible way Jim had treated him at the New Year, pushing him under the mud.

"I'd have leathered his backside if I'd known!" rumbled his father, and his mother said *she* had never taken to him.

When she heard the news Marion Stewart raised her hands in horror. "Oh! isn't that terrible. Did you hear the latest, Mother?"

When the old lady finally understood what her daughter-in-law was so eager to tell her the "Terribles!" went zooming round the little kitchen like bluebottles round a carcass in July. Old Kenneth came in at that moment from the byre.

"What's going on here?" he asked irritably. "What are you cackling about, Marion, like a hen that's laid an egg? Well, out with it!"

The story came tumbling out. Marion was sure that even Grandpa, odd as he was, would have to agree with her this time. The effect was not what she had expected.

"Sarah in a pool of blood!" bellowed the old man. "Hasn't she been asking for it ever since the day—and a bad day it was—they came here? Who put the dogs on to our Ayrshire cow till they drove her into the river and broke her leg and made her lose her calf? And when Gran'ma's best tablecloth was hanging out of their cow's mouth, all green with slime, and Peter—he was only a lad then—ran to save it, who came after him with a stick for touching her cow? Eh? Was it Sarah? Aye, it was, and a bad neighbour she's been all these years. What! Not a word to say? You were doing plenty of cackling just a minute ago. They could hear you on the road!"

Marion tried to stand up to him but when he stood glaring at her she gave in. "Oh! Gran'pa," was all she found to say in a patient "I'm better than you" kind of tone.

"Aye! you like fine throwing blame on other people but you don't know what happened. Likely she goaded him too far—I don't know—nor does anyone else, but if I see the boy I'll help him, and if anyone else in this house sees him they'll keep quiet about it. Is that plain?"

"It's not right, Gran'pa!" Marion protested, for this was breaking the law, but he stood there, every hair of his beard bristling, and she lacked the courage to go on. She turned tail and could be heard sobbing up the stairs.

"What's the matter with Marion?" quavered the old lady, not having followed these heated exchanges.

"Got the hiccup!" grunted her husband, settling down for an evening's read of the newspaper.

The police came next day and searched every house, barn, byre, and henhouse till they came to Big Kenneth's.

He met them on the doorstep. "Have you a search warrant?"

"No, Mr. Stewart, I have not," replied P.C. Macleod, "but I'm sure in the interests of law and order——"

"You'll not put a foot inside this house, or the barn, or the byre without a search warrant, Constable Macleod."

The policeman recognised defeat when he met it and walked back to the road where the two Bruces were waiting for him.

"Are you not going in?" Donald cried.

"I can't do a thing without a search warrant," explained the constable. "Now, if I had thought in the morning—but who would have expected the old man to put obstacles in my way?"

Donald reported this to Sarah a few minutes later, saying, "He is a poor creature! He is afraid to go into a house unless they let him. Such a man is no use to us!"

" They're all against us! " said Sarah, propping herself up on one elbow, her great eyes fixed on Donald. " The boy's there, then! Bad neighbours they've been to us! "

From outside in the passage Finlay groaned a response.

When the constable returned from searching the forester's house the Bruces told him that he must go to Brae. Macleod's heart sank. Brae! there and back a five-mile walk and only his bicycle to carry him home at the end of it. A wild-goose chase, too, the boy was being hidden by the Stewarts at Corrie; that much was clear.

" He'd never stay by himself! " he suggested.

" Is it not the very place for a man that would murder his foster-mother? " cried Donald, at once becoming excited. " We will get a boat and cross the loch before he escapes."

At the mention of a boat Macleod brightened. The three of them dragged out a boat and with Macleod and Finlay at the oars pulled out from the shore.

Tom had had his eye on them and now raced up the hill to a vantage point from where he could train his father's spy-glass on the cottage. At first all he could see was a blur; he had focused too hastily. " Bother! " he muttered. " Bother! Oh! let him see them coming. Don't let him be caught! " Suddenly he had the little house clearly before him. Nothing moved, there was no face at the window. This cheered Tom immensely till it occurred to him that Jim might still be in the house. If he was he could not get out unseen for the hill to which it clung lay bare to anyone approaching by sea. If he was indoors he was trapped. Meantime, the boat had gained the shore, two men got out, clambered up the steep path. Tom could hardly bare to watch. They disappeared indoors. Would they come out dragging Jim between them? Tom's heart was beating uncomfortably fast and his elbows ached from leaning on them, but he did not dare to shift in case he lost sight of them. There they were! Coming out! Only two! Tom gave a cheer and rolled over on the turf.

Hurrah! they hadn't got him. When he looked again they were coming away from the barn and making down to the boat. "Hurrah!" he shouted, startling a couple of hoodie-crows. He rolled on the grass and buried his face in a clump of moss sniffing up the nice, earthy smell. Then he jumped to his feet and ran for home. When the Brae expedition passed back he was busily sawing driftwood. They tramped past in silence, the clump, clump of their tackety boots ringing on the cobbles. That, too, faded and only the faint conversational murmur of the hens vied with the squeak of the saw.

The final search was made at Corrie next day but Jim was not there.

"He must be out of the island!" sighed the policeman.

"He is not!" declared Donald. "Did you not tell me there were no boats missing!"

"He's at the Lodge," said Finlay. "They are hiding him as they did last time."

The crofters kept their own counsel. To begin with they had talked of nothing else but now no one said a word either for or against. The wind whined about the houses at night, showers lashed against the window panes, dogs whimpered to be let in out of the wet. The women shivered. Was the boy out there in the cold and the dark? Even those most against him at first said nothing now. But often they could be seen straining their eyes, searching the far side of the loch. Donald Bruce had found his old army binoculars and stood at the corner of his house training them on Brae.

"He was in the Lovat Scouts," Charlie Grant said casually, nodding in the direction of the distant figure.

"Has there been any sign of him, Charlie?" asked his wife and he knew she didn't mean Donald Bruce. He hesitated, then shook his head. Safer to say nothing but the fact was that the cattle, Alasdair's cattle, were never down near the young trees. Even when they were half-way along the loch at nightfall and

you might reasonably expect them to keep on and reach the
trees by morning they never did. Instead they could be found
up in the Corry Mor or even on the hill past the Brae cottage.
The forestry workers remarked on this among themselves but
said nothing at home. Women were not to be trusted. Murdo,
carting fencing material, heard all this and worried about the
boy. Was there still enough food up in Brae? In a way it was a
pity the police had not found him for he was sure that Jim was
not guilty of very much. But on the other hand the Bruces
might calm down and ask him to go back. It was difficult,
Murdo thought, to know what to do for the best. He decided,
however, to take food over and that very night he landed a big
bag of supplies on the rocks below the house when he, Dan, and
George were out fishing for cuddies.

Tom waited up for his father that night. He was half asleep
by the dying fire when the sound of fish being slapped down in
the sink woke him.

" Did you get many, Dad? " he asked, struggling out of his
chair.

" A few, a few, it was a fine night."

" Dad? " Tom stood beside his father, looking at the fish,
their colours dulled in death, their eyes glazed over. " Can I go
next time? "

" Go fishing? Aye! of course, if you want to——"

" No! to speak to—to—Jim." He brought the name out
with difficulty; no one had used it for days.

" They're watching," Murdo said. " They've got the glass
on the place all the time. Give this boot a tug, boy, get it by the
heel." Tom grasped the wellington by the heel and pulled
hard.

" But at night, Dad? "

" Charlie was telling me they were up and down the path
at night. Pull harder, boy, or I'll have to go to bed in my
boots."

Tom gripped the obstinate boot and this time succeeded in dragging it off.

" He'll be hungry."

" I left some food in a bag."

" I could cross by boat. He'd like to see me, I know."

" I'm sure he would but best leave it a little time, lad, they'll calm down—they won't keep this up for long."

Tom wasn't so sure. Worried and unhappy he went up to bed. Jim would think he had forgotten him, Jim would think he did not care.

Jim did think just that. He had been alone so long he had lost count of time. When he had first fled to Brae he had pictured Tom coming over and together they would plan what was best to do. Alone like this he couldn't think. Nothing was clear. He didn't know where to go nor what to do. He had handed over to Alasdair the money for the bullocks and had only what was left of the pound Alasdair had given him. Would the police keep on looking for him? Was Sarah dead? If she was, would they hang him? These questions went round and round in his head, round and round, but no one came. His eyes grew tired watching, but every night he risked walking after the cattle and turning them when needed away from the tiny trees. He was very careful, indeed, doing this, keeping off the path and listening intently every few yards.

Gradually, as his loneliness became more acute, he went farther till he could see the lighted window of the forester's house. It drew him like a magnet. This night he determined to reach it, come what might. He had become as quiet as a cat in the dark and gained the window unseen. The curtains had been carelessly drawn and through the gap he could see the forester sitting with his feet up, reading the paper, and his wife knitting a sock. It was a commonplace sight but, to Jim, it spelt heaven. His heart ached inside his chest. What if he just walked in and threw himself on their mercy? They had been kind to him before when he and the baby shared the birthday cake and they had praised him. Now he was an outcast and no one cared what happened to him. He could die of cold and hunger and it was all one. He hesitated, his longing to hear a human voice battling with his fears. He took one step towards the door and at that very moment his sharp ears warned him of footsteps. He had just time to flatten himself against the wall when he heard Donald's dry cough. He was carrying a lantern, its light wavering a little way ahead, but leaving the night beyond all the blacker in comparison. Jim blessed his stars that his eyes had grown used to the dark. Donald was now between him and Brae but he could work his way back quietly by the shore. He moved away from the house, all thought of giving himself up completely banished from his mind. It was easy to follow Donald's progress by the light of the lantern but he, himself, slipped like a shadow from rock to rock, keeping a short distance behind. How far would Donald go? If he reached Brae he'd find Spot and plenty of other things to show he had been there, but he won't catch me, he thought, exulting in his own powers.

At the cross-roads the light halted. Jim sat down to wait. Presently he saw the flicker of a match, then the whiff of tobacco came on the breeze. It was a nice, familiar smell. Donald would sit, Jim reckoned, till he'd had his smoke so Jim must stay put. He did not dare to risk the slightest sound, even the fall of a pebble, while the other sat so quietly. A few stars showed their light through a ragged scarf of cloud.

Donald got to his feet, spat, and turned homeward. Jim, down below, grinned as he listened to the tramp, tramp of his feet receding in the distance. If they wanted to catch him they'd need to be a little wider awake than that! The encounter cheered him up and he hurried back home to supper. Spot was waiting for him and gave him a warm welcome.

"Hush, now, quietly does it, old boy," said Jim. He talked to the dog as to a person. It made him feel less lonely. "We'll

put on a fire, eh? And then supper—but the window first." He
pinned a blanket over the window and then lit the fire with his
last match. He was glad when the sticks caught and crackled
merrily. Next he considered the state of the larder.

"What about herring, Spot?" The dog's bright eyes were
fixed on the boy's face with an unwinking stare. "Not herring?
Porridge, then? All right, and we'll put butter and cheese on
the scones we found this morning. Yes, you'll get your share,
same as mine." While he was talking he made the porridge,
then he got the scones, buttered them, and filled them with
cheese. His mouth watered and so did Spot's which reminded him

of their journey in the guard's van. "We don't have to sit and watch him stuffing himself to-night, Spot, do we?" So saying, he offered the dog a scone. It went in one gulp, and Spot pricked his ears in hope of more. Jim shook his head at him. "Aw, take your time, man. I'm going to make mine last." Which he proceeded to do, chewing each small mouthful a long time. Yes, he decided, it must have been Murdo who left the supplies. He had been caught unaware by the boat and if it had been policemen they would have nabbed him. The time they *had* come over he had been high on the hill and had watched the search as if it had been a play put on for his benefit.

He poured the porridge into two bowls telling Spot he would have to wait till it cooled.

"I'll give you another scone but *don't* gobble it." Spot did, however, and had a long wait. Jim sprinkled the last of the sugar on his own portion.

"Well, that was a bit of all right," he told Spot, "but we can't cook another time because we're out of matches. It doesn't matter, though, because Alasdair is sure to be here soon and then we'll be all right." He got up, yawned, and stretched. "Come on! Bed!"

The two outlaws made themselves comfortable in Alasdair's bed. At first Jim had kept Spot on the floor but when one night he had found him lying at his feet he hadn't the heart to push him down. They slept soundly.

There was no one awake to see the boat glide into the narrow channel between the rocks below, no one to see three figures climbing the steep path. Then Spot woke, burst into a volley of barks.

"Quick, run!" Two of the men sprinted the rest of the way, barged into the house. Spot, by this time, was quite frantic, inside the bedroom. As soon as the door opened he sprang on the intruder and buried his teeth in his hand. The man cried out and hit the dog on the head. The beam of the torch showed a boy raising himself on one elbow, his face blurred still with sleep.

" That's him! Get him! " Dragged out of bed, Jim put up no resistance. A dreadful feeling of doom had him in its grip. This had to happen. There was no escape.

" You'd better come quietly, no nonsense, mind, or we'll handcuff you. Tell that damn' dog of yours to keep off! "

But Spot was not looking at them. He had his eyes on the door, whining gently, his tail giving a tentative wag, and then Alasdair walked in.

" Oh! Alasdair——" burst from the boy. " Oh! Alasdair, don't let them take me."

But Alasdair said nothing. " We've got him! " one of the policemen said.

" Alasdair! " Jim's voice implored him. The drover, his features sharp in the torchlight, looked at him then.

" You did a terrible thing, attacking your mother."

" Alasdair! I didn't—you don't understand——"

" I understand well enough. You hit your foster-mother and left her lying, not caring whether she was alive or dead. That's enough for me."

" You'll be making a report on any damage he's done to your property. Let me have it as soon as you can so that——"

" No! I will not! I'm not making any charge," said Alasdair harshly. " Take him away! "

The policemen hustled him outside. He kept stumbling, the night was pitch black. Somehow they reached the boat. He sat huddled, not looking or listening. Alasdair had come as he had hoped but Alasdair had turned against him. There was nothing to hope for now.

17. In the Hands of the Law

Murdo and Alasdair Bàn sat together on the back seat of the bus. The seats were made of wood, the roads were rough, full of pot-holes, springs were none of the best, and they were well shaken. It was difficult to talk over the roar of the engine and the rattling and groaning of everything movable in the interior.

But Murdo, unlike his usual calm self, insisted on talking.

"Maybe it wasn't like that at all!" he kept saying, to which Alasdair kept replying:

"How else could it be? Didn't Donald himself tell me the minute I set foot in Udale that night. The way he told me I thought he was *there*!"

"You can't believe everything they say," replied Murdo. "Och! it's not easy for you—you haven't known them the way we have over the years. If the least thing goes wrong it's somebody else's fault."

The bus was climbing a steep hill in low gear.

"What? What? I can't hear you."

Murdo waited till they had gained the crest of the hill and then repeated his remarks, adding, "If they found a stirk in a bog they'd be sure at once that someone put it there."

Donald Bruce, in the front of the bus, turned to glare at Murdo. What was he doing there, anyway? The Procurator-fiscal hadn't sent for *him*, but he had added himself to the party. He was up to no good, that was certain. Donald beckoned to Alasdair to come and sit behind him but the drover had his

hands on his knees and was gazing at the floor, his mind in a
state of unwonted confusion. Had he been too hasty and blamed
the boy for something he had not done? But Donald had sworn
to him that he was telling the truth, he had even made it look as
if he, Donald, had arrived in time to witness the attack. Now
Murdo had thrown doubt on all this. If the boy had not done it
then he, Alasdair, had been too hasty. Of all things he hated
being in a state of doubt. He liked things to be black or white.

The Procurator-fiscal sat in his long, narrow office listening
to one witness after another. He was a small, stout man, bald
save for a fringe of red hair round the nape of his neck. He was
seldom seen to look directly at anyone yet his grey eyes missed
little.

The Bruces, both in their Sunday best, had done their utmost
to blacken Jim's character.

"You couldn't believe a word he said, your honour," said
Sarah. "Not a word! I was always on to him to tell the truth
but it was worse he was getting, not better."

In the silence the clock on the mantelpiece ticked loudly and
a coal fell down in the grate. The Fiscal, seated behind a broad
desk strewn with papers, examined his hands.

"Did he refuse to work on the croft?" he asked. Donald
took over.

"He worked, right enough, your honour, but it was that man
that told him to." This grievance came out with a rush and at
once Sarah joined in.

"He would do anything Alasdair MacAskill wanted and I
told *him*," she nodded to her husband, "how it would end if he
didn't put his foot down, but he wouldn't listen to me and he
let the boy go with the drover and see what happened!"

Donald shifted uncomfortably on his hard chair. Events had
proved his wife right. It irked him to think he had gone and
bought clothes for the ungrateful scoundrel and the pair of boots
still on the kitchen dresser near broke his heart. Was there any

chance the shopkeeper would take them back? They hadn't been used and . . . He came back with a start to the matter in hand as he heard the Fiscal say to his wife, " Thank you, Mrs. Bruce. Just one or two questions to your husband—you were out fishing the night of the alleged attack? "

" I was, sir, me and my brother, Finlay."

" When you came home what did you find? "

Donald opened his eyes wide. Surely the man knew all about this part of it already? But the law was always strange.

" My wife, sir, was she not lying in a pool of blood and moaning and groaning, something terrible? "

" What did you do? "

Donald leant forward earnestly, saying, " Why, I ran to her, sir, asking her what had happened."

" And what did she say? Can you remember her exact words? "

" Yes, I can, sir, though I could hardly hear her for she wasn't speaking clear like, but I knelt down and put my head close, that way I could make her out. ' Jim,' she said. ' Find him, Donald, he bought me a present '."

" ' He bought me a present.' You are quite sure your wife said that? "

" Oh! yes, sir, I was so frightened I can never forget."

The Fiscal turned back to Sarah who was staring at the floor.

" What present did he bring you, Mrs. Bruce? "

" A box of chocolates for me——"

" Yes? "

" And——" her voice dragged. " A pipe for Finlay and a stick for *him*." She shot Donald a vindictive look.

" He had some thought for you when he brought home those gifts? "

Sarah gazed blankly at him for a few seconds, then she broke out wildly, " No! No! He had no thought for us. He was just covering over his being away so long. It wasn't chocolates I wanted, it was obedience. I told him he was to go no more to Brae but to do the work for those that kept food to his mouth and clothes to his back and I sent him to his room——" Here she broke off and began rocking herself backwards and forwards.

Donald said softly, " Hush! now you're not to take on."

The Fiscal examined his fingernails. " You sent him to his room. Did he go, Mrs. Bruce? "

Sarah moaned, her mouth working, " He always did what I told him, he always did——"

" And this time, Mrs. Bruce? "

" He ran at me, he hit me! Why are you asking me all these questions? You know all this, you don't need to be asking questions."

The Fiscal rose to his feet saying, " I'm sorry I've upset you, Mrs. Bruce, you've been most helpful. Take your wife for a cup of tea, Mr. Bruce."

The Bruces left, Sarah leaning on her husband's arm, and Miss Menzies came in. She made short work of Jim; he was a difficult pupil, dour, sullen, inattentive.

" You had often to punish him, Miss Menzies? "

" Oh! yes, sir, I strapped him very often for spilling ink on the girls' clothes, talking and damaging school property."

" You have doubtless had some experience of mischievous boys, Miss Menzies. Would you say that Jim Smith was any worse than the average? "

" Up to a year ago I didn't think so," she replied, after a moment's thought, " but last winter he had a queer way of looking at me and I remember saying to Mrs. Mackenzie where I lodge that I'd be glad when he left. It was just a feeling I had but he used to bully the younger children."

" This man, MacAskill, influenced the boy very much, it appears. For good or for bad, would you say? "

The teacher hesitated, then replied slowly, "For good, I suppose, but the thing was that no one existed for Jim after Alasdair came and that galled his foster-parents."

"Thank you, Miss Menzies, you have been most helpful."

Kursty Morag came next, round and rosy, breathless from climbing the long stair. She described Mrs. Bruce's injuries, a cut under her kneecap, a bruise on her face, and another cut on the bridge of her nose. "It was that which caused all the bleeding," she went on. "Sarah's—I mean Mrs. Bruce's—nose always bled very easily, oh! the least tap and it would bleed for hours with her trying cold keys down her back——"

"And the cut under her knee?"

"Well, sir, seeing as how the boy had turned on her, it could have been done by his boot."

"Supposing you hadn't known about the boy what would you have thought, Mrs. Macdonald?"

"Well, sir, I must say it reminded me of the time I tripped over a herring box in the dark and got cut just there, quite deep it was, too, and took a long time to heal."

"What was the state of the scullery?"

"State!" exclaimed Kursty Morag, raising her hands on high. "As sure as I'm here, sir, it took me an hour to get it decent like—down on my knees scrubbing—perhaps I shouldn't be running on like this, but you'll excuse me, sir, I was never before a sheriff in my life——"

"You are not in a court of law, Mrs. Macdonald. Just give me your impressions in your own words. I am not yet taking formal evidence. What made the scullery so dirty—blood?"

"Well, yes, sir, there was blood, right enough, but that scrubs off easy. It was the chocolate, it was trampled into the floor and Mrs. Bruce was all smeared in it, even her hair was all matted. I had a job washing it out and her carrying on all the time. There must have been a terrible fight, sir, and no wonder she was upset."

A policeman showed Mrs. Macdonald downstairs where she found Miss Menzies waiting for her. Over the tea cups they thrashed out the whole subject.

" A nicely spoken gentleman," said Kursty Morag, " but it was me that was pleased to get out of that building! If you think of all the trouble that boy brought on the township, the whole lot of us having to come all the way from Udale in a special bus! I'm sure it will be in Borstal he'll land."

Meanwhile Alasdair MacAskill was sitting in the chair vacated by Kursty Morag. Still in a state of doubt he confined himself to answering the questions put to him. Yes, Jim had taken the cattle on by himself to Dingwall and had done very well—and a flash of the old Alasdair here—" But I had him well trained, your honour." Yes, he had handed over all the money. Alasdair had always found him both biddable and reliable. He had gone back to school and never missed a day more when he, Alasdair, had taken him in hand.

The Fiscal sat toying with a paper-weight. The silence made Alasdair feel even more uncomfortable.

" What were your feelings when you heard of this accusation, Mr. MacAskill? "

" Well, your honour, it was the way it came on me, sudden like, and the way Donald Bruce told me, I thought it was all true——"

" And now? "

" Now I'm not so sure. I believe there was no one there but the two of them."

" Exactly, Mr. MacAskill, and the trouble is the boy won't speak. Don't go home just yet. I may wish to see you later."

The Fiscal sat on playing with the paper-weight, shifting it from hand to hand. Clearly there were two boys in trouble, not one. The first was dour, sullen, mischievous, a liar, a bully, a potential thug. But the other was reliable, honest, determined, faithful, and courageous. The Fiscal sighed. Downstairs in the sergeant's house lay the first boy, refusing to eat or speak. But where was the other boy?

Well! one more witness. He rang the bell and Murdo Mackenzie came in, carrying his cap in his hand. He stood awkwardly just inside the door breathing heavily. The room felt unbearably close and stuffy.

The Fiscal welcomed him. "It was good of you, Mr. Mackenzie, to come all this way of your own accord. I shall be very glad to hear your views. I confess I'm puzzled and the boy won't say a word."

Murdo nodded his head thoughtfully. "That's because Alasdair turned against him."

"Sit down!" said the Fiscal, shooting him a quick glance which Murdo noticed.

"Och! yes, sir, Jim thought the world of Alasdair Bàn. He'd do anything for Alasdair."

"I see." The Fiscal paused and then went on. "Had the boy any other friend, one of his own age, say?"

"Oh! yes, your honour, my son, Tom. He's been worrying over Jim. He gave me no rest till I said I'd come and tell you that Jim never did it. He isn't like that, my Tom says. I don't know, sir, I wasn't there, but Sarah, Mrs. Bruce, I mean, hadn't a nice way with children. You've got to have patience with them when they are young. Tom's heard her going at Jim when he was a wee lad, no higher than two hens, and she'd egg the men on to beat him——"

There was silence in the office. One tiny tongue of flame leapt out from the well-drossed fire. The Fiscal lit a cigarette and waited. Murdo wrestled with the problem, twisting his cap round and round in his large red hands. "It's this way, sir," he said at last. "I have a mare—she was badly broken in for the man who had her before me kicked her and beat her if she didn't understand at once what he was after. She was just about ruined for work by the time I got her. She was that nervous she'd bolt for a feather crossing her nose. She would put her ears back expecting me to lay into her for months after I got her though I never used a whip. At last she saw I wasn't going to, no matter what tricks she tried so then she gave up her nonsense and now she's a grand worker."

Murdo paused, disturbed by the way things were going. All this talk about a mare! The Fiscal would be calling a policeman any minute and he hadn't got to the point yet. Well, he must finish it now.

"It's this way, sir. Jim was badly handled like my Sally. He needed firmness but he needed kindness, too. He was almost always hungry, he was cold in the winter, and he was beginning to feel his own strength. Then Alasdair came along and he knew how to handle him—it's in a man or it isn't, I often think. Well, Jim would do anything for Alasdair, as I was saying. If he'd asked him to walk off the end of the pier he'd have done it. Well, I mustn't waste your time, sir, but if there was someone proper in charge of him Jim would make a fine man yet. That's just what I came to say—my Tom says he didn't do it."

The Fiscal rose and thanked him warmly. "You haven't wasted my time! You've been a great help and I think I shall want to see you again."

So there it was. Had he the whole picture now? He thought so. Downstairs Jim was told to get up.

"The Fiscal wants you!" said the sergeant's wife. "Now don't be sullen. You'd much better own up and plead guilty and get it over for if you don't you'll have a long time to wait before the court sits. Brush your hair, for goodness' sake! I'm sure I've done my best for you, doing your washing, even that filthy shirt you had on, but small thanks I get!"

Her words fell on deaf ears. Jim followed the sergeant upstairs and was shown into the long, narrow, stuffy room where he had been questioned so many times already that he had lost count. They could go on questioning him to Doomsday, he

would not answer. Plead guilty? What did that mean? Or
plead not guilty? They said he could have a lawyer if he wanted
one. That was funny, thinking he'd want a lawyer!

He stood looking blankly at the worn carpet till told to sit
down. After a pause, as if orders were reaching him from a long
way off, he sat down. He began counting the squares in the
pattern of the carpet for he had discovered for himself that if he
kept his mind busy doing something while he was being
questioned then he hardly heard what they were saying. He had

reached the fortieth square when it struck him that the bald-headed one had not opened his mouth and that was odd for he had been a great one for asking questions. There were forty-five squares the long way. He'd have to count the next side more slowly to make it last. He wished the man would get on with it.

"What present did you bring home for Tom?" The question came suddenly and Jim's head jerked up. Surprise chasing the closed-in look off his face he stared at the Fiscal.

"You bought Tom a present. What was it?"

"A bicycle pump." Jim's voice was little above a whisper.

"Where is it?"

"Up in Brae."

"She didn't take it from you?"

Jim shook his head.

"She spilt the chocolates, she broke the pipe and the stick——"

"No, she said they'd beat me with the stick," Jim corrected him.

"And then she took the pump or tried to?"

Jim nodded.

"How did you rescue it?"

Jim was back in that awful scullery. He saw Sarah dragging out the big pot, he saw her bringing down the pump on the rim, felt himself leap over to save it, and relived the struggle, swaying now forward now back over the chocolate-coated floor.

"She was too strong for me—I couldn't get it away—but it was *my* pump. I paid for it in Dingwall. Then she tripped over the pot, she struck her face. She looked up at me, blood pouring out of her nose. I knew if she got her hands on me she'd kill me so I ran. That's all."

"Was the pump very much spoilt? Will you still give it to Tom?"

Questions! Questions! Questions! You answered one and

they came at you with another half dozen! Jim looked angrily at the Fiscal.

"How can I give him the pump when I'm here and the pump is—is——" He choked suddenly and turned his head away.

The Fiscal picked up papers on the littered desk, put them down again, hunted in drawers, and finally scribbled notes on a pad. Then he said, "Tom sent his father here to say that he knew you didn't hurt your foster-mother, despite appearances. I think he'd like to get the pump, don't you?"

Jim would not look at him. "It was spoilt," he muttered, and stopped short, the tears he had not shed in all those days running down his face. He sniffed and having no handkerchief, rubbed his eyes with his sleeve.

"It's all right," said the Fiscal irritably, "it's all right, you don't need to cry *now*. There won't be any court case, there is nothing against you. We shall take steps to find you a new home."

"Borstal?"

"No, certainly not. Who put that idea into your head? I mean a real home where you can work and be happy."

Jim tried to listen to what the man was saying but, having at last given way to tears he found he could not stop. He sat and wept, regardless of all else.

18. A New Life

Mary Martin was making preparations for her visitor. There had been much coming and going over the last few days, official cars stopping at the roadside much to the curiosity of the neighbours. The Fiscal himself had come bringing with him Alasdair Bàn and Murdo Mackenzie and they had filled the little kitchen but Mary took it all quite calmly.

"Of course I'll have the boy," she said. "He's not like a stranger. I saw him already with Alasdair—Mr. MacAskill," she corrected herself for the benefit of the Fiscal and the importance of the occasion.

"We've discussed it many times," he had said. "It will be better, we feel, for everyone that the boy should not go back to Udale as he might be a cause of strife. Of course, it will be only temporary while Mr. MacAskill is looking for a good place for him and his board and lodging will be paid."

"I would do it, anyway," Mary said, "for he ought to get a chance."

The Fiscal had shaken her warmly by the hand and told her father they were most grateful to them both. His final words to Alasdair had been to search for work for Jim with all diligence, and to let him know as soon as he had found it.

And now Jim was coming. His bed was ready and Mary had been busy making cakes and had white and black puddings for tea.

She saw the police car stop and the boy get out. The car turned and drove off. She ran down the road to meet him.

"Oh! Jim, I'm pleased to see you," she said warmly and led

214

him to the house. "Here's Jim, Dad!" The old man rose and shook Jim solemnly by the hand. Jim was very silent but the awkward pause was filled by Mary chatting as she made the tea and soon they were all seated at table.

Mary had looked forward to seeing Jim eating a huge tea as he had done twice before in her house but she was disappointed. He ate very little and did not seem to care what was offered.

He sat silently by the fire afterwards watching the flames. When Mary said he was probably tired and would like to go to bed he got up at once and followed her to the room.

Mary expressed her disappointment to her father. The old man ruminated for a little over his pipe and then said, " It's the being in prison, it changes a person."

" But he wasn't in prison, Dad, just in the sergeant's house."

" He was a prisoner—he couldn't get out. He'll take a little while to g t over it."

Mary thought it over and realised that her father was right. Too much had happened to the boy in too short a time. They must have patience.

The slow days passed. It was a quiet time of year, the only work left to put the rams to the hill. The cows fed on the croft on the green grass where the hay had been gathered. The potatoes had been lifted and stored in clamps. The weather itself was quiet—no sun, no wind, no rain. Morning mist hung on the hills and the loch lay quiet as a mirror.

Mary cudgelled her brains to find jobs for Jim to do. She sent him to the shore for driftwood and made him saw what he brought home. She asked him to clean the byre and to scrape the paths clear of the summer growth of weeds and grass. He did everything with the same listless air and when he had finished sat down once more by the fire. Sometimes she caught him watching the kitten in the basket. Against all probability it had stayed alive.

"I gave it milk out of a fountain pen filler," Mary told him.
"After that the teaspoon was no use. But I never really thought
it would live and just look at it now!" The kitten was making
a very gallant attempt to purr. "Do you think it'll ever learn
to lick its own coat? They say they don't learn unless their
mothers teach them."

But Jim had lost interest and did not reply.

Then one day, just at dusk, Alasdair breezed into the house
in his old way, assured of a welcome which, indeed, he got but
not from Jim. The boy sat in silence on the settle and would not
look at him. There were all the usual questions as to people's
health and then Alasdair came out with his news.

"I've found a job for you, Jim, it's just the work that will
suit you. Mr. Mortimer's a great friend of mine, I've met him
at all the sales, so I wrote him and he's needing a boy. The farm
is called Blairmor, about eight miles out of Dingwall." He went
on talking about the farm, the livestock, and the people for some
time and it was only when Mary brought in the lamp that they
saw that Jim had disappeared.

"He'll be back in a minute," Mary said. "I'm sure it's grand
you've got him a place! Not that we want to send him away but
there isn't enough for him to do and he's wearying."

"There'll be plenty for him to do there and he'll learn. I
wish I'd had such a chance when I was young."

He stayed talking for an hour waiting for Jim but he did not
come back. He rose to go.

"Will you not make a *ceilidh*, man?" grumbled John.
"We haven't heard the half of your news."

But Alasdair was in a hurry to go, he had to see a man about
heifers he was half thinking of buying, he had been so busy
over Jim's affairs lately he had had no time for his own.

Jim was sitting up on the hillside, his two arms round Spot's
neck. He had found him sitting on the doorstep and had enticed
him away up the hill above the house.

He sat now murmuring into Spot's ear, "You were the only one to help me, Spot, old boy, you bit the man's hand—he had a bandage on it for days and every time I saw it I thought of you. You didn't desert me."

The night was very still. They heard quite clearly the noise of the front door opening and then Alasdair's voice floated up; he was commenting on the weather, it was grand for the sheep. Spot came to attention but Jim hugged him the closer. "You stay with me, Spot," he whispered. Then came Alasdair's whistle, sharp, piercing. Spot whined and struggled to get free. "No! No! You stay! I'll feed you, we'll go away together." But the dog began to yelp. "Oh! go on, then," cried Jim, loosing his grip.

Spot disappeared in one bound and presently Jim could hear Alasdair rebuking him. "And what were *you* playing at?" Spot barked joyfully in reply and then the noise faded away in the distance. Jim got to his feet. He was growing chilly, he'd have to go in. But if they think I'm going where *he* says, well, I'll show them!

Mary was in quite a state. Alasdair had waited and waited for him. What had he been doing? "And look, Jim, what he's left! Money! And I'm to buy you clothes. He says you gave him such a hand with the cattle last year that you earned it. I'll get you clothes to-morrow. They're wanting you next week, Jim, so we haven't much time."

Jim let her run on. They could buy him clothes, he had earned them, and he would go away but not to Blairmor and not to look after cattle, he was finished with that.

Jim was cleaning the byre next day, carrying out the first graipful, when he heard a shout.

"Hi! Jim." And there was Tom getting off his bike. Jim had just time to notice the pump in its proper place before he sloshed the dung on to the dung-hill and went back in for more.

By the time he came out Tom was standing by the door, smiling all over his broad, freckled face.

"What are you doing here?" Jim asked.

"I've come to see you."

"You have, have you? You've taken long enough."

Tom considered this carefully. "I'm working with the Forestry now so I only have Saturdays free."

"Huh!" was all Jim answered before disappearing once more into the dark interior of the byre. Tom heard noises of a hoe scraping the drain.

"I'll give you a hand," he offered, preparing to take off his jacket.

"Don't bother," was the only answer and then after a pause a muffled, "you don't need to come here at all."

"I wanted to come."

"You could have come last Saturday."

"We were dipping the sheep."

It was a simple explanation but it made Jim only more angry. He scraped away at the cobbles outside the byre, using so much force that he struck sparks from them with the hoe. Then he rounded on Tom.

"Well, maybe you were, but what were you doing when I was up in Brae? What made you so busy then?" His dark eyes were fixed on Tom's face and saw him flush.

"I wanted to go but Dad said it would make things worse."

"Who for?"

"You."

"How?"

"They'd know you were there for certain; they were watching all the time."

"Didn't they know anyway? Didn't they come anyway?" Jim asked him scornfully, his face dark with anger, but Tom shook his head resolutely.

"No, we didn't know that. Dad thought they'd calm down

after a bit and call the police off. They were sure to want you
back——"

Jim glared at him. "A likely story! You can't even tell a
decent lie!" He placed the hoe carefully against the wall and
took a step towards Tom as if he meant to strike him. "I'll tell
you how it was," he said bitterly. "All you wanted in Udale was
peace and quiet. The Bruces could do just as they liked, murder
me if they wanted to, not one of you would move a finger!
When I did get away last winter your father took me back,
telling me it would be all right—oh! it would be just grand!
Well, was it? Was it? You haven't much to say now, have
you? You're such a good boy, you do everything your Dad tells
you. You never gave me a thought up there alone. You were
some friend——" He broke off to bash at a clump of nettles
with his boot, and then resumed, "I'll tell you how it is—you
just want rid of me so he—*he*—(his voice betrayed anguish) gets
hold of that farm at the back of beyond and he plans to pack me
off there. I'll be well out of the way and they can take a horse-
whip to me without anyone being a penny the wiser. You'll all
be cosy together in Udale!"

"Och! Jim," said Tom. "Talk sense. Dad doesn't care
tuppence about the Bruces, if they're pleased or not. It's you
they're thinking of. You can't go back with *them* and you need
a job."

"I could stay with you and work on the Forestry."

"But you always said you'd never work on the Forestry!"

"Well! I could have worked with Alasdair Bàn," Jim persisted. "But no one cares—you just want to see the last of me!"

"Honest, Jim, it's not that way at all! Alasdair's been doing
nothing else but looking for a place for you. He said he couldn't
keep you himself, that it's taking him all his time to keep going
the way prices are. I heard Dad say to Mum afterwards that he
thought Alasdair wouldn't stay long in Brae, anyway. He's
always been restless, going from place to place sudden-like the

way he came here and not liking being tied down. But he was down every day looking for replies to the letters he got her to write——"

"Her? Who?"

"Miss Menzies."

"What!" cried Jim, shaken out of his resentment for a moment. "She didn't write about me?"

"She had to! Alasdair said the letters must be just right and he wasn't good with a pen himself. The first place they got, the wee man in Portree said it wouldn't do because you had to sleep in a bothy."

"I wouldn't mind a bothy."

"Well! *he* wouldn't hear of it and Alasdair had to start all over again. The funny thing was that Miss Menzies was telling Mum she was tired of it, she wasn't going to put pen to paper for him, not any more, but when he came in and asked her she never said a word, but took out her pen and that blue pad she has."

Jim listened to all this with amazement. He had been so lost in misery he had never thought there might be another side to the story.

"Aye!" said Tom, chewing on a straw. "Mum says she's sweet on him."

This was too much! Jim grabbed the hoe and had another bash at the nettles but it struck a hidden stone and the head flew off the handle, landing yards away in a wilderness of dockens.

"Oh! gosh!" exclaimed Jim and ran to search. Tom followed, giggling so much that Jim had at last to laugh, too. "It's no joke, though," he explained, "for the old boy's awfully careful about all his tools."

"I've got it! You'll need to slit the top of the handle and then hammer in a wedge. That way they'll stay."

Tom had taken out his knife while talking and they set about the operation together. By the time the head was firmly fixed they were back on their old cordial footing.

"Anyway," said Jim, taking up the conversation where they had left off, "I'll bet he's not sweet on her!"

"Och! I'm sure he's not," replied Tom, straining truth for once, but not wanting to see the hoe head part company from the handle once more. "Sarah's gone."

"What!" This new item so startled Jim that he quit the byre and went to sit on the stackyard wall.

"Aye! she's gone. Her sister came for her in a car and took her away. Donald and Finlay are that touchy they go off like kegs of gunpowder. There was a row in the fank. Peter Stewart

221

was dragging a ewe to the dipper and without meaning to he bumped into Donald. The next second Donald had his fist doubled under Peter's nose."

" And then your father stopped the fight! "

" Not this time. Peter was too quick for him. He got Donald one blow on the chin which sent him backwards into the wall. Finlay set up such a caterwauling you'd have thought he was hit himself. The two of them went away shouting they'd have the law on us but the boys were laughing so much we could hardly make them out."

Jim listened fascinated. It was great to think someone had hit Donald hard. But Sarah gone! That was almost unbelievable. Why, she had never once left Udale in all the years he could remember. Now that life which he had always known and which had seemed as fixed as the great cliffs which guarded the entrance to the loch had toppled and vanished like a dream. Only a year ago he had felt himself a prisoner in a fortress. But his struggle to keep a pump had made it collapse like a pack of cards.

" Tell me all about Dingwall and the cattle," Tom said. Jim came back from far away. Tom was still there, Tom as he had always known him. He knew now that Tom hadn't let him down and some of his resentment drained away. He smiled and began. They were still at it when they heard Mary calling that dinner was ready.

" Come in! Come in! " she said to Tom. This was the first meal Jim ate with real appetite and it did Mary good to see him.

Tom stayed till late and when he was going he said, " I'll see you in Dingwall, Jim. Mum has a sister there and she says I can go at New Year when we get a few days."

Jim mumbled something. Inside his head he was saying, " I'm not going near Dingwall, we won't meet."

" That'll be fine! " Mary cried. " Jim's sure to get a few days then, too, and he can show you round."

Tom was putting on his coat and didn't notice anything odd in Jim's silence.

The last evening came all too soon for Jim. Now that his time was running out he wanted to stay. Mary was bustling about between the kitchen and his bedroom, packing his new clothes into a case of her own. She had bought him shirts, a pair of trousers, and dungarees.

"You'll need to buy yourself a winter coat with your first wage," she said. "I hadn't enough, but that place will be cold after the New Year."

She came through with one of the new shirts and put it to air beside the fire for he was to wear it travelling. Jim began to feel more and more uncomfortable. This business of disappearing was all right when you felt that everyone had let you down. It wasn't so easy with Mary doing so much for him. She had washed and ironed his old clothes and now she sat down to darn a hole in one of his stockings. He paced up and down, his inward discomfort growing stronger every minute.

Just then his eye fell on the kitten curled up in its box on a bed of rags. From far off Alasdair's words came back to him. "She was always looking after lame puppies and lost kittens."

Before he could stop himself he said gruffly, "You're good to me because you think I'm like that kitten!"

Mary looked up at him, the needle arrested in its weaving. She looked from Jim to the kitten and then she smiled.

"No, Jim," she replied, "I never thought of you that way. I'll tell you what I think. You'll grow up to be a fine man. Because you've had things hard you'll be able to feel for other people. You'll be a man that people will trust."

Jim flushed to the roots of his hair. "Do you mean that?"

"Would I say it if I didn't mean it? It isn't every boy of your age would go all the way to Dingwall——"

"And then he turned on me!"

"Yes," she agreed, facing the trouble. "He's too hasty, he

always was, and then Donald didn't tell him the truth, but he's been trying to make up for it ever since. Don't be too hard on him, Jim, we all have our failings. When we're young, we think older people are all strong but it isn't so."

"I wasn't going to go!" he blurted out. "To that farm, I mean. I thought they were just trying to get rid of me."

Mary went on darning comfortably. "You were upset and no wonder! You give the farm a try, anyway. Maybe they'll be nice people but if they're not just you come straight back here and Alasdair can start looking for something else. There'll be an open door for you here."

Mary's kindness melted the last of Jim's hard feelings.

"I'll go," he said. "I'll give it a try. Maybe I'll learn a bit there and there'll be sales quite handy."

"Yes! and come home here when you get a holiday."

Home! Jim looked round the little kitchen, cosy and warm in the lamplight, the flames leaping up to the kettle hanging on the great hook. Yes, it would be home to him now and yet he had just passed weeks in it wishing he were somewhere else. He smiled ruefully. You wanted something all your life but when it was there for the taking you didn't even notice!

The kitten woke up, mewed, rose to its full three inches, and mewed again. Jim grinned at it. Mary might deny it but he knew at that moment that there was a very real bond between him and it. They had both been rescued, the kitten from death and he, himself, from carrying a load of hate and resentment all his life.

Now he would go away believing in himself because Mary had faith in him.

"Will you feed him, Jim, while I get supper?"

"Yes," said Jim, smiling and picking the tiny creature up. "I'll feed him."